"YOU WOULD NEVER MARRY SUCH DULLNESS."

Susannah twisted her hand in his grip, but could not break his hold. "How can you say that?" she demanded. "You don't know me."

"But I do." He released her hand and captured her chin.

"No," she gasped, recognizing his intention.

Warne leaned nearer. He wanted her mouth under his, her slim, taut body closer still. "It is not safe, is it, Susannah Bowen?" he whispered.

"You are forgetting the thief," she reminded him.

"You make me forget."

Avon Books are available at special quantity discounts for bulk purchases for sales promotions, premiums, fund raising or educational use. Special books, or book excerpts, can also be created to fit specific needs.

For details write or telephone the office of the Director of Special Markets, Avon Books, Dept. FP, 1350 Avenue of the Americas, New York, New York 10019, 1-800-238-0658.

An Improper Widow

KATE MOORE

AVON BOOKS ◆ NEW YORK

AN IMPROPER WIDOW is an original publication of Avon Books. This work has never before appeared in book form. This work is a novel. Any similarity to actual persons or events is purely coincidental.

AVON BOOKS
A division of
The Hearst Corporation
1350 Avenue of the Americas
New York, New York 10019

Copyright © 1995 by Kate Moore
Published by arrangement with the author
Library of Congress Catalog Card Number: 94-96263
ISBN: 0-380-77542-5

First Avon Books Printing: February 1995

AVON TRADEMARK REG. U.S. PAT. OFF. AND IN OTHER COUNTRIES, MARCA REGISTRADA, HECHO EN U.S.A.

Printed in the U.S.A.

RA   10   9   8   7   6   5   4   3   2   1

For Mom and Dad

Acknowledgments

I would like to thank my mother's cousin, Ms. Betty Kirby, of Highcliffe, Dorset, for providing me with replicas of the 1810 Ordnance Survey for southern England and for researching Susannah's dream cottage in Wincanton. It is really there. And I would like to thank Joan and Tracy Grant, aka Anthea Malcolm/Anna Grant, for their help with innumerable research questions including the vexing issue of "marquis" vs "marquess." And, of course, Homer, for his inexhaustible inspiration.

The son is rare who measures with his father.
                                        —*The Odyssey*

1

Francis William Arden, fourth Marquess of Warne, entered the breakfast room of his house on Upper Brook Street on a wet March morning, knowing he would find Cornelius Bellaby ahead of him and wondering how he was to tell his friend that he had decided to marry.

Bellaby looked up from the *Chronicle* at Warne's entrance. "Raining is it?" he asked.

Warne nodded. "Buckets."

"Thought it would" was Bellaby's reply. He bent his ginger-colored head to the paper again without further comment, as if the sight of a peer of the realm, unshaven, sweating, and dressed in a sleeveless shirt and white stockinet breeches, was no more remarkable than a flying pig.

Warne smiled. There was hope for Bellaby after all. At first his friend had objected strenuously to Warne's habit of taking a morning run. "You'll pollute your lungs and shrink your privates," Bellaby predicted. In time, however, as neither Warne's health nor his manhood had suffered, Bellaby had been compelled to accept the eccentricity. Now Warne hoped his friend would accept his decision to marry.

He picked up the fresh towel draped across the back of his usual chair and applied it to his wet hair. He rubbed briskly for a moment, then discarded the towel and wrapped a forest-green robe around his white running clothes. He chose an orange from a plate on the sideboard and crossed to the window.

Beyond the rain-dappled glass an old soldier shuffled by to take up his post at the crossing. Warne had first noticed the man several days before and had given him a shilling for performing his self-appointed sweeping task. It was these old soldiers returning to take up lives interrupted by the long war with Boney that had started him thinking about marriage. His war, too, was over. This season he could take a wife.

"Warne, here it is, just the opportunity we've been looking for." Neil Bellaby stabbed the small advertisement in the *Chronicle* with his forefinger and lifted his gaze from the paper, but his friend appeared not to have heard him.

Warne was staring out the window apparently deep in contemplation of some object visible only to himself. Bellaby noted his friend's inattention. It reminded him that it was an accident that he and Warne were friends—the corn merchant's son and the peer. He clenched his jaw firmly shut. He wanted to plead with Warne—*don't change*—but of course, he would do no such thing.

For nearly ten years they had begun the day perusing the papers, making sense of the details of shipping, trade, and foreign affairs that revealed economic principles at work and showed them their next venture. Warne's breakfast room—the idea room, Bellaby liked to call it—had become their meeting place after a successful venture had allowed Warne to purchase a town house. It was

Warne's quick intuitive flash that spotted the opportunities that had made them both rich. Bellaby was the detail man. Now, however, something was distracting Warne from the pursuit of wealth. Bellaby felt a moment of cold fear that his friend would never play the game again with the brilliance that had been so exciting to watch over their years as partners.

Outwardly, Warne looked the same. His auburn hair hung loosely about his face, carelessly toweled and still damp. He ran regardless of weather. The tall, powerful body retained that look of leashed energy that made women of a certain stamp eager to bed the marquess. But Warne's face had changed. The blue eyes were more often amused than angry. He laughed more readily. He pushed his enemies less hard. He looked younger than he had a year ago. Warne was no longer at war.

It had been Warne's hatred of his father that had fueled his drive for wealth, that much Bellaby understood. When they first met, Warne had been penniless, living by his wits and his athletic prowess. Bellaby had had a fortune in furs from Canada and boundless admiration for the disinherited young peer with his quick fists. They had become partners. Then on the very day Wellington had beaten Napoleon, the old marquess had died.

Since then Warne had assumed his father's title. He had taken his seat in the Lords and made his maiden speech, a speech in which he had painted a vision of England's manufacturing might. He had told the peers of his father's era that with their investment England could produce steel as she now produced muslin and then all the veterans of the war could be employed. For his pains he was dubbed "The Iron Lord," and a caricature appeared in print shop windows showing Warne's dying father borne into the streets on an iron bed.

Warne turned and caught his friend staring. "Sorry," he said. "You found a mill for conversion?"

Bellaby blinked and allowed a slow grin to stretch his mouth wide. Warne had been listening after all. "Paper mill, seven acres, not far from Kennet's canal. Price is right. Shall we go take a look?" He thrust the *Chronicle* into his friend's hand, and stood. On the wall behind him several sheets of the *Ordnance Survey* had been pieced together. The huge map was dotted with pins indicating the location of various Warne properties and businesses belonging jointly to Arden and Bellaby. Whenever he could, Warne had purchased property adjacent to one of his father's estates and bettered it. Bellaby searched for something near the mill in question and found a small property near Wincanton that could serve as a headquarters. He put his finger on the spot.

Warne studied the few lines describing the advertised mill. They had been looking for an enterprise that could be run entirely by steam. This could be it, but the conversion would mean spending months in Somerset, overseeing the work of engineers and craftsmen. After a pause, he suggested, "You go, Neil."

Bellaby's wiry frame tensed. "I will, of course, but I thought you were particularly interested in this project."

"I am, but I have another . . . project here in town."

His friend's face fell, and Warne realized he had blundered badly. "Not a business project," he hastened to explain. "I would never act without you in business, Neil."

"Well, what then?"

Warne met his friend's piercing blue gaze. "I am going to . . . marry." He almost said *re*marry, but he had never told Bellaby the story of his first marriage and the tale was best forgotten now.

"Marry!" Bellaby's mouth fell open, and his right hand, raised to point out some spot on the map, fell. He took a few purposeless steps as if to distance himself from the idea, whirled, and strode back. "Who?" he demanded.

"I don't know," said Warne. "I've got to pick somebody. That's the project." He reached for the bellpull and rang for his butler.

"Why?"

Warne had to laugh at the utter incomprehension expressed in the one syllable. "Why marry? So that when I pass to my immortal reward or punishment as the case may be, four hundred years of Warne lands go to a Warne instead of Prinny or his heirs."

"You have a point there," Bellaby conceded. "Prinny never could handle money. In his hands even your fortune would dry up." Bellaby was pacing in earnest now.

When the butler appeared, Warne asked, "Do I have any cards of invitation lying about, Pedrick?"

"Of course, sir. Would your lordship care to see them?"

"Straight away, thank you."

"Sir," said Pedrick, "may I mention that there is a gentleman waiting to see you, a Mr. Inkson from Lett's."

"Lett's? The stationers?"

"Yes, sir."

"Send him in."

"Marriage . . ." Bellaby said with a shudder. "This is what comes of your damned monkish habits. Running, celibacy."

"Celibacy?" By the standards of the day Wayne knew himself to be restrained, but his lapses had earned him a reputation that years of abstinence would hardly erase.

Bellaby snorted. "Well, how you manage without a mistress, I don't know. I'd say you're as randy as the next fellow."

"As the proverbial goat at any rate," Warne acknowledged. He tossed the paper on the table and helped himself to coffee.

"That's my point, Warne," Bellaby insisted. "Make an arrangement with some accommodating piece and leave it at that."

"As you have with the patient Alice?"

"Exactly. Alice could find you a prime article."

Warne shook his head. His distaste for such arrangements went beyond his rebellion against his lecherous father.

"A widow then, an improper widow, one who knows what's what under the sheets."

"No, it's a wife I want."

"You aren't thinking of some chit right out of the schoolroom! You'll be obliged to come to her in the dark, keep your nightshirt on, and apologize for offending her sensibilities when you enter her."

"Bellaby, trust me to pick a bride who will welcome my attentions."

"You'll never find one at that temple of dullness—Almack's." There was a moment of silence. Both men knew that the Iron Lord would not be particularly welcome at Almack's.

"You'd do better at the Mansion House. Let a few plump aldermen parade their daughters before you. Look at their teeth as well as their bosoms and demand thirty thousand in the bargain."

"With all due respect, Bellaby, I want a wife with better manners than you have."

"You want a paragon, then?"

Warne sipped his coffee. He had considered this. He could not go looking for a girl like Ellen Kirby, the girl he had married when he was seventeen. "Wit and goodness, passion, a little beauty will do for me."

"Lord." Bellaby ran a hand through his hair. "You want to fall in love."

Warne tried to recall Ellen Kirby's eyes. For years he had remembered his love with painful clarity, and then inexplicably, when he was winning, when he was finally repaying his father for her death, the memories had faded. "I doubt I can," he told Bellaby.

A knock on the breakfast-room door cut off Bellaby's further objections to Warne's marriage plans.

Pedrick ushered in a thin gentleman with a wide brow sparsely covered with fine yellow hair. The gentleman rolled his head from side to side as if his thoughts were too weighty to be supported by his slender neck. "Mr. Inkson, my lord," Pedrick announced, stepping aside and discreetly setting a silver salver of cards at Warne's elbow.

Mr. Inkson looked from Warne to Bellaby, and Warne followed the visitor's gaze. Bellaby, magnificent in a blue coat, yellow waistcoat, and white inexpressibles, looked every inch the Bond Street Exquisite, while Warne sprawled in a chair in his green robe. His visitor's mouth opened, but no sound came out.

"He's the peer," said Bellaby with a laugh and a nod toward Warne.

"Seat, Mr. Inkson?" invited Warne.

"Yes, thank you, my lord," Mr. Inkson replied. He sank into a chair as if his legs had just that moment given out.

"Coffee?" Warne asked.

Mr. Inkson shook his head. He had retained his hat and turned it around and around in his hands by the brim. Warne waited.

Mr. Inkson cleared his throat and rolled his head to the right. "My lord, I came to report a most curious circumstance. Most curious, indeed."

"Yes, Mr. Inkson?" Warne prompted.

"It came to my attention this morning that our shop had been robbed during the night. A person or persons unknown removed a pane of glass from one of the windows at the rear of the shop, turned the latch, and contrived to enter." Mr. Inkson's heavy head listed to the left.

"An unfortunate occurrence. Have you suffered a severe loss?"

Mr. Inkson's head came upright, and he opened and closed his mouth like a fish. "In fact, your lordship, no monies were taken and only one item is missing from our stock, and that is why I have taken it upon myself to wait on you."

"Yes?"

Mr. Inkson's heavy thoughts caused his head to lean to the right again. "My lord, your cards have been stolen. I assure you we can print a new order immediately and have them to you within three days, but I wanted to advise you of the theft lest someone perpetrate a fraud in your name. One of the cards was left behind." Here Mr. Inkson paused, laid his hat upon his knees, and reached into an inner pocket of his coat. He drew out a small creamy card bearing the marquess's name and title and handed it across the table to Warne.

Below his name was written in the neat hand of a very careful student—*With my father's compliments.*

Bellaby saw Warne's eyes assume the iron look that had not been there since the old marquess died. He came around the table and peered over Warne's shoulder. "Someone's playing a joke," he said.

"A nasty joke," said Warne. He rose, and Mr. Inkson popped up like a cork on a fishing line.

After some pointed questions about Lett's handling of the matter, Warne requested Mr. Inkson's discretion and offered him the customary parting civilities.

Mr. Inkson bowed and backed from the room. In the hall Pedrick could be heard directing the visitor to the door.

"Queerest theft I've ever heard of," said Bellaby.

Warne studied the message on the card left behind by the thief. He could swear he had seen the handwriting before.

"You don't think it's a joke, do you," Bellaby said.

"Revenge, more likely. *No score left unpaid* was my father's motto."

Bellaby frowned and slowly circled back to his side of the table. "Could be one of your father's men. They went down with him, you know."

Warne was thinking the same thing. His father's man of business, his solicitor, his bailiff were all men who had remained loyal to the old marquess. They had suffered with him as Warne succeeded. Probably, Jopp, his father's banker, felt sufficient enmity on his own to act against Warne. He would investigate Jopp first.

"Bellaby, this episode is another reason for me to stay here. The thief can hardly use my cards while I'm in town."

"Very well," Bellaby replied. "I'll look into the paper mill, but I ask one thing of you."

Warne raised an eyebrow.

"Before you get yourself leg-shackled, I want to meet any lady you are considering."

"You've never presented me to the fair Alice." Warne named the young woman Neil had in keeping in a house in Kensington.

"Of course not," said Bellaby from the door. "While my lady swears she's partial to freckled fellows with ginger hair and wiry builds, I'd rather not put her to the test, Warne."

2

Susannah Lacy kept her mittened hands folded and her eyes respectfully lowered, grateful that she had put on her bonnet and pelisse before Uncle John had sent for her. She watched a little puff of her own breath rise and drift away on a current of cold air. At least there would be rugs in the chaise. And, in London, Lady Lacy would overheat all the rooms of her house. Uncle John often complained that his estranged wife was guilty of just such extravagances. *No fires before nine, no fires after nine* was the rule in Baron Lacy's Berkshire seat, even here in the library where her uncle was frequently at work on estate matters as early as seven.

She heard the scratch of his pen stop and felt his gaze on her. Her glance shifted briefly to the folds of her dove-gray kerseymere skirts and the intricate swirls of the crimson Turkey carpet underfoot.

"Now miss," Uncle John began. Susannah did not look up. "You will wear your cap at all times."

"Yes, Uncle John." A needless reminder. When had she been tempted to remove her cap?

"Any vanity of person or dress ill becomes a woman in your position."

"Yes, Uncle John." Susannah tried to picture herself in silks and diamonds, flaunting her beauty

11

before the *ton*, and failed. Skinny and brown, with dark hair and eyes, an overwide mouth, and no bosom to speak of, in a ballroom she would hardly draw the notice of her fellow chaperones.

"You will remember your duty to your charge and your indebtedness to this house."

"Yes, Uncle John."

"You will remember who sheltered you in your hour of disgrace and who has provided your support for ten years with no other return for my charity than such small services as you have been able to render this house."

"Yes, Uncle John."

She would be more grateful if Uncle John congratulated himself less often for the charitable impulse that had led him to take in his ruined niece as an unpaid governness to his children.

She heard him rise and come around the large desk that dominated the dark room. He stopped in front of her, and that was her cue to look up. Uncle John was a spare man and not overly tall, and though she was not tall herself, not as tall as her cousin, Juliet, Uncle preferred to have Susannah seated looking up at him rather than standing and meeting his gaze.

"I do not scruple to tell you, miss, that chaperoning Miss Lacy will be a difficult task. Your charge will be reluctant to heed your advice, as the young inevitably are reluctant to hear sense. And her mama . . ." Here Uncle John paused to control his temper as he always did when he spoke of his estranged wife. " . . . her mama will want to indulge the girl's every whim and encourage dangerous romantic notions. London itself induces folly in all but the most prudent of natures." He frowned. "You have the list of Miss Lacy's eligible suitors?"

"Yes, Uncle John," Susannah began counting. She rarely escaped an interview with her uncle before a dozen *Yes, Uncle John*s.

"The three gentlemen I have approved will call upon you. I have asked Lady Lacy to prepare a list of suitors she favors for Juliet as well. Get those names to Drummond and Drummond immediately. I want the fortune hunters and fribbles eliminated as quickly as possible."

"Yes, Uncle John." Susannah was surprised that he had thought to ask his wife's opinion at all, but, of course, he did not intend to consider any men Lady Lacy thought fit for her daughter. "And, if my cousin, if Miss Lacy, finds some young man not on the list to her liking?"

"See that she does not. Submit all her callers' names to Drummond and Drummond at once. They will know how to expose the mercenary motives of prospective suitors."

"Yes, Uncle John."

He looked sharply at her as if he suspected her of irony. "No doubt some would say that sending you to oversee Miss Lacy's come-out is the height of folly, but I think not. I think you know the frailty of woman so well and have paid so dearly for your own sins that you must be the most vigilant guard of Miss Lacy's reputation and the most ready to insure that she fixes the attention of a man of rank, fortune, and steady character."

Susannah took a deep breath. "We do have an agreement, Uncle, and I will fulfill my end of the bargain. Have you written up the terms as I requested?"

Uncle John said nothing to her. His icy blue eyes, pursed lips, and rigid stance answered Susannah's boldness. He turned and reached for a paper on his desk, which he held out to her for her inspection. The document promised that Susannah Lacy, also known as Mrs. Susannah Bowen, would upon the day of Miss Juliet Lacy's marriage to a suitable *parti* receive one thousand pounds and title to Shady Lane Cottage, Wincanton, Somerset. Susannah noted with relief that in witness thereof Mr. Kilvert, the vicar, had signed his name. "Thank you, Uncle John," she said.

He waved away her thanks with an impatient hand. "It is all very well to make provision for your success, niece, but mind you, I make no provision for failure. Should Miss Lacy's reputation suffer in any way, should her mother's influence lead her astray, should you succumb a second time to the weakness of your own nature, there will be no refuge for you here. And do not imagine that either of your brothers will be willing or able to take you in."

Susannah bit her tongue and dropped her gaze. It would be senseless to make the rebellious reply she was longing to make. Whatever the difficulties of chaperoning her lovely young cousin through a season, at least in London she would be spared Uncle's priggishness.

A knock sounded at the library door. "Papa," came a sweet voice from the other side, "may I come in?"

The door opened even before Baron Lacy gave his consent, and a young woman in a celestial-blue cloak and matching bonnet entered. Juliet Lacy favored her mother in appearance. She was taller and fairer than her cousin and endowed with a magnificent bosom. Titian curls framed an oval face. Blue eyes passed curiously over Susannah as they had more and more often of late.

To Uncle John's credit he had never once men-

tioned Susannah's disgrace to his children. To her
charges she was their widowed cousin, Mrs. Bowen.
But Juliet, admitted at eighteen to adult gatherings,
showed a new consciousness of what had not been
said about Susannah. With the instinctive sense of
the young for any weakness in those placed over
them, Juliet had begun asking questions about
Susannah's past.

"Am I interrupting?" Juliet asked now, with
another sidelong glance at her cousin.

Susannah rose and smoothed her skirts.

"Not at all," said the baron. "I was just giving
your cousin some instructions about your suitors,
miss."

Juliet frowned, her sweet mouth contracting in a
pout. "How tiresome for you, cousin."

"Entirely necessary," said the baron. "Your cousin is to see that you remember what you're about,
my girl. Your mother will have you dancing til
dawn and haring off to one rout after another, but
see that you pay attention to the gentlemen that
count."

"Oh, Papa, trust me, I'll have my pick of the best,
I know it."

Susannah lowered her eyes lest they give away
her opinion of that bit of conceit.

"Now, Papa, it's raining, and the horses are standing. Coachman says we must be off. Do let us go,"
Juliet pleaded.

Her papa's face softened, and he took his daughter's arm, and led her out. Susannah followed, firmly closing the library door.

"Susannah," said Juliet, breaking a silence that
had lasted since luncheon, since Susannah had
refused to allow her charge to observe a mill in

progress across from the inn where their horses were being changed. "Do you think this is Hounslow Heath?"

Susannah pulled her hands from under the lap rug, rubbed a clear spot in the condensation on the glass, and peered into the gloom beyond the carriage windows. Though the rain had stopped, clouds still covered the sky, bringing an early dusk. The carriage lamps threw a moving patch of light across the road, illuminating little more than the ruts of other coaches. "I can hardly see a thing," Susannah confessed, "some gorse, I suppose, and a copse or two. It could be."

"Don't you think that's famous?" inquired Juliet. "To be passing such a notorious spot on such a dark, forbidding evening?" She gave a little shiver. "What if we should meet a highwayman?"

"I trust Coachman and Tim Dachet will know what to do," said Susannah. "Tim Dachet's pistol will discourage any villains from thievery."

"I swear, Susannah Bowen, you were never young," Juliet complained.

"Possibly not," Susannah replied, as if it were not the most profound lie. She tucked her hands back under the warm rug.

"*Possibly not, nevertheless, I trust so*, you don't even argue properly, Susannah. How am I to endure the season in your company? You'll spoil everything, I know it."

Susannah pressed her hands together. If she wished to have any success in managing her charge, she must be patient. "What exactly will I spoil, Juliet?" she asked.

"Everything . . . my reputation for fashion. How can I be seen with you? You are always in brown or gray. You never have the least neckline, always a ruff or a tuck, no jewels, and those hideous caps."

"Then you may be certain that the eyes of all the gentlemen we meet will be on you," Susannah replied, refusing to be drawn.

"Hah, and what will these gentlemen say to me with you sober as a funeral hovering near? No one will flirt or laugh."

"Neverthe—"

Coachman called out some imprecation, and the coach rocked with a sudden slowing of the team. Susannah braced herself, and Juliet grabbed for the strap, turning first to one window, then the other in a plainly futile effort to penetrate the darkness.

"Do you think we are being held up?" Juliet asked.

"Apparently, and I don't think it's the least romantic," said Susannah. She could not be seriously alarmed. Tim Dachet was a stout fellow, and he had protected them all day, even in the crowds of unruly gentlemen about the mill.

Abruptly the coach halted. They could hear the gruff voice of Coachman, and before the carriage had stopped swaying, Juliet pushed open the door and poked her head out into the night.

"Juliet, don't," Susannah cried.

"Juliet, do," said a male voice.

And Juliet did, pushing the steps down with her foot, and descending from the vehicle in a rustle of skirts.

"'Arise fair sun and kill the envious moon . . .'" said the stranger, in a deep, rich voice that an actor might envy.

"Fair sun?" Juliet asked.

Susannah laughed in spite of herself. Apparently they'd been stopped by a highwayman as romantic as her young cousin. With a sigh Susannah threw off the lap rug and stepped out into the raw evening after her cousin. She looked up at the highwayman, who was staring at Juliet. "Your lines are wasted on the young lady, sir, as she was wont to rebel against memorizing in the schoolroom."

"Oh," said Juliet to the stranger, "you're quoting. What is it?"

"*Romeo and Juliet*, of course." The highwayman sounded a bit surprised and younger than Susannah had first thought.

Susannah could just make him out now, a cliche in a great coat, mask, and tricorn hat, sitting astride a fine black horse. She could not see a weapon in the dark, but that did not mean he was unarmed. She turned to their protectors and saw only Uncle John's old coachman.

"Coachman?" she called. "Where's Tim?"

"Fool Tim Dachet's gone and fallen off the box," came the reply.

"Where? How shall we find him?"

"About a hundred yards back, ma'am," the stranger told her. "Actually, I assisted him a bit in the fall. I dinna' wish to have him fire that great pistol of his. He landed in the gorse, and I suspect he'll catch up to us in a moment. So I must beg a boon of you while I can, ladies."

"A boon, sir?" Susannah replied. "After such a rude interruption of our journey, after knocking our protector off the box? A boon would be appropriate had you rescued us rather than inconvenienced us."

"My apologies for any inconvenience, of course, but haven't I rescued you? Have you not been rolling along dull as a Sunday sermon since Staines, hoping for an adventure, which I have been so kind as to provide?"

"Oh yes, however did you guess?" asked Juliet. 'We have been wishing for an adventure all day, but I have no boon to give you."

"I can think of a fair one—a kiss."

Susannah gasped. The clouds parted slightly and a bright moon outlined the figure of the man on horseback and the girl staring up at him in open admiration. And suddenly Susannah saw the true danger of the situation, for she remembered being just as young and foolish as her charge. "Juliet, no," she ordered.

"Don't be stuffy, Susannah," said Juliet. "It's just a kiss, and I am not afraid. It's an adventure, after all." She stepped up to the stranger, and the highwayman leaned down. Susannah could think only of putting an end to this dangerous association at once. She strode forward, raising a hand high to slap the rump of the young man's horse. But the highwayman guessed her intent and drew back, urging his stallion into a quick side step.

He laughed, and told Juliet, "You are well guarded, my lady."

The sound of approaching hooves made them all turn.

This would end it, Susannah thought. The company of other travellers would dispel the romantic aura that seemed to have caught both Juliet and the stranger. Susannah called out at once, "Halloo, help, a highwayman!"

The hooves pounded closer, and the masked young man, after only the briefest hesitation, said, "Adieu, my lady Juliet," whirled his horse, and galloped into the copse.

Two men also in greatcoats and tricorns rode up immediately, but when they halted at the Lacy carriage, Susannah felt her relief give way to cold fear. The newcomers reeked of ale.

"What have we here, Dick?" said one rider to the other, over the blowing of their lathered horses. "Sport or goods?"

"Looks like sport to me, George," said the second rider.

Susannah decided to ignore the implications of this exchange. She had often surprised her charges into good behavior simply by stating with conviction her expectation that they meant to be good. "Gentlemen," she said, "as you can see, our coach has been waylaid. We would be grateful for your assistance and would be happy to repay your kindness when we reach London."

This speech was greeted by harsh laughter that sounded ugly on the empty heath. "That's what we like. The work done for us." The first man drew a pistol, while the second slid from his horse and advanced on the two ladies.

Susannah took Juliet's hand and pulled her back from the approaching ruffian.

"This one looks plump as a partridge, George," said the man. The strong smell of sour ale washed over them as he spoke. "You fine ladies have any jewels about you?" he asked.

"No pearls to cast before swine, if that's what you mean," Susannah said.

"Hah, Dick, pearls afore swine, a wit that one," said the man on horseback, and he went off into his peculiar harsh laugh.

"Crack your wit on me, will you," said Dick. "I'll crack you." He raised his arm.

"I wouldna' if I were you," came the first highwayman's voice from the shadows behind the two robbers. Dick's hand froze in mid-air and the robber on horseback swung his gun toward the voice. A shot rang out, and the rider shrieked and dropped the pistol. "I'm hit, Dick, let's give it up. It's a bad lay."

Dick stared at Susannah and Juliet, apparently undecided. Then a new sound caught their ears, a long, low groaning, like a lion in pain.

"Come on, Dick," urged the injured robber.

Dick hesitated a moment longer, then spat as if to mark the scene with his contempt. He snatched up his partner's fallen gun and scrambled toward his horse. The two would-be robbers rode off as fast as they had come.

The low groan came again, and Juliet and Susannah turned to the sound.

"Tim Dachet, is that you?" Susannah called.

"Ooooh, me head," came the reply. There was a rustle in the bushes, and Mr. Dachet staggered toward them, holding his head.

For a few minutes Susannah and Juliet ministered to their injured protector, offering their handkerchiefs to wipe the cuts and scrapes on his face. Coachman grumbled at Tim's lack of wit, but gave him a restoring sip from his flask.

Then the highwayman spoke again. He had emerged from the shadows as they tended Tim and now stood in the road, holding his horse's reins. "Ladies, I'd like to see you on your way. Can your guard regain the box?"

"Sure I can, no thanks to you," said Tim roughly.

Juliet whirled toward the stranger. "You did save us," she whispered fervently.

Tim Dachet squared his shoulders, swayed slightly, and staggered toward the box.

The young highwayman stepped up to Juliet, though Susannah noticed that he avoided the pool of light cast by the carriage lamp. "I think your friend . . ."

"My cousin, Mrs. Bowen . . ."

"Your cousin would say that I brought you into
danger in the first place. I beg your pardon. That
was not my intent."

"Of course not. You intended something high
and romantic, a rescue from tedium," Juliet assured
him.

Susannah groaned, and the highwayman
laughed. "I will claim that boon of you then,
Miss . . . ?"

"Lacy," Juliet told him candidly. "I will gladly
give you the boon for which you asked, sir."

"No," Susannah protested. She stepped between
her cousin and the young highwayman. "Sir, think
what you are about. You may harm Miss Lacy
much more by stealing a kiss than by robbing her
purse."

"Susannah," wailed Juliet. "You don't understand."

"Pardon me, Miss Lacy," said the highwayman.
"I mean neither harm nor disrespect." He reached
inside his cloak, and Susannah tensed, wondering
if he meant to draw his pistol again. "If the propri-
eties won't allow me a kiss, let me leave you my
card." He held out a small white card that showed
faintly against the black of his clothes. Juliet stepped
forward, but the highwayman held the card out of
her reach.

"Into the coach with you, Miss Lacy," he urged.

Susannah did not need daylight to recognize the
sulky cast of Juliet's features, but the girl complied
and Susannah followed.

The highwayman doffed his hat and presented
the card with a bow. Juliet snatched it and held it
close. The young man closed the door and sprang
back on his horse, and Coachman cracked his whip.

"Adieu, my lady Juliet," came the highwayman's voice drifting back to them from the heath.

Juliet breathed a soft sigh, and Susannah knew it for the first breath of love, against which reason, propriety, and regard for worldly advantage, all that she was charged to keep in her cousin's mind, would be powerless. It was going to be a dreadful season.

3

On the evening he began his search for a bride, Warne dined at White's with his brother-in-law, the earl of Rumsford. Rumsford, twenty years Warne's senior, had married Lady Cassandra Arden when Warne was ten, and their marriage had produced a degree of felicity with which neither found fault.

With the covers cleared and a good claret to sustain them, Warne revealed his intention to marry.

"Ah, that explains the satin knee breeches," said Rumsford referring to Warne's evening clothes. "Going to look over this year's crop, are you?" he asked.

"I thought I would try the duchess of Somerset's ball," Warne replied. He had called on his sister's friend Maria Sefton that afternoon, and she had recommended the duchess's ball.

Rumsford nodded approvingly. "Too bad Cassandra is in Bath. She could tell you about this year's girls. Remarkably good information she has. Daresay Maria will look after you."

Unspoken was the awareness that Warne's welcome in society would not be warm. "Thanks, Rumsford, but I will manage," he replied.

"Or some gel will manage to snare you, Warne," said his brother-in-law with a chuckle. "Did I tell you about my Alice? Picked Moreton out at a

Venetian breakfast. Might have been buying a bonnet." At a slight smile from Warne, the earl launched into the anecdote.

He had hardly reached his point when another man stepped up to their table with an abrupt movement that cut Rumsford off mid-sentence.

"Maitland," Warne said, acknowledging the newcomer, a tall man with sleek dark looks and the tight-lipped intensity of the offended.

"What is the meaning of this, sir?" demanded Maitland. He threw a card at Warne, and the stiff rectangle of white paper landed face down on the table.

"Evening, Maitland," said Rumsford, quietly reminding the newcomer that civility was called for.

After a pause Maitland managed a curt, "Evening."

Only then did Warne pick up the card and turn it over, though he knew what he would find—his own name and the enigmatic message—*With my father's compliments.*

"Where did you get this, Maitland?"

"Where did I . . . where did . . . as if you did not know, Warne. I will have satisfaction for this," Maitland said grimly.

"For a card?" said Rumsford. "Surely a gentleman may leave his card without giving offense."

Maitland glared at Warne. "Not in the bedroom of another man's mistress."

Warne tried to recall whether he had heard the name of Maitland's current *cher amie.* The man consumed partners with the same voracious appetite for sensual indulgence that had marked Warne's father.

"In this instance, Maitland, I am as puzzled as you are. Who is it you have in keeping these days?" Warne asked.

"Do you deny a connection with Diana Ferris?"

Diana Ferris. Warne had not seen the "Fair Ferris" for years. It was a shocking measure of her decline that she had taken up with Maitland, who no doubt beat her. Warne felt his muscles tighten and the hot bitter taste of anger on his tongue. For a mad moment he considered giving Maitland the satisfaction he demanded. With one shot Warne could free Diana. But he was done with bitterness. With a bank draft he could probably do as much for his former lover.

"My connection with Miss Ferris is past, Maitland, and that someone has had the bad taste to remind her of it is not grounds for a duel."

"Someone!" Maitland was choking with his rage. "This is your card, Warne."

"My dear Maitland, this is *Warne*," Rumsford interposed, as if he had explained everything. He raised his brows and shook his head at the younger man, as if to say, *This is the Iron Lord, the man who ruined his own father.*

Maitland appeared struck by Rumsford's expression and for the first time seemed to waver in his conviction that Warne had poached on his preserves. Warne had to admit there were certain advantages to his reputation. Carefully he put the card on the table.

"Did Miss Ferris tell you I left my card with her?"

Maitland's glance shifted away. Warne could see that the other man wanted to conceal whatever had happened between himself and the woman. Diana Ferris was most likely laying compresses to her bruised face even as they talked. Warne's hands closed in fists.

"The card arrived with a bouquet of roses for

Miss Ferris this morning," Maitland said tightly.

"That's what she told you?"

There was a silence as Maitland apparently weighed his next words. "That's what her maid said."

Warne rose without ceremony. "Then very likely, it's true. Excuse me, Maitland, I have an engagement this evening."

Warne turned to Rumsford and took a cordial leave of the older man. Without a backward glance he left the club.

"You had best watch where you leave your cards, Warne," Maitland shouted, but too late. Rumsford could not be sure the marquess heard the other man at all.

By the time Warne reached the duchess of Somerset's, he had decided on a sum he thought Diana Ferris would find useful and a friend who could be trusted to convey a bank draft to her without arousing Maitland's suspicions. He found himself sobered by the thief's rapid and malicious use of the stolen cards and perplexed by the strange message.

In the duchess's receiving line he tried to resurrect the optimistic spirit in which he had set out to find a bride. He bowed over Her Grace's hand, accepted her austere delight that he had come to her ball, and moved with the press into the ballroom.

His sister's friends acknowledged him, but he was conscious of the distrust of most of his fellow guests. He had initiated an economic battle against one of their own, and his success had brought down many. The print shop caricatures of him suggested the Iron Lord used unfair tactics. No one seemed to understand how he had marshalled his money like troops against his father's interests. Small sums at first, then as the wealth had increased, he had wanted it to produce things as land produced crops. He had sown money and reaped cloth and paper and iron. And the iron had gone to fight Napoleon, but now he could do with it as he wished, and he wished to build bridges and buildings and machines, great engines that pulsed with life and never tired.

Two hours into the ball he was wondering whether he might simply advertise for a bride and interview likely candidates. Or perhaps Bellaby was right, and he should seek an improper widow for an affair. He had seen many *ton* beauties this night, but none had moved him. They seemed like his hostess's hothouse blooms, showy and forced. If another young woman said, "La, sir!" to him, he would not answer for his actions. He lifted a glass of champagne from the tray of a passing footman and took a stand with his back to a fluted Corinthian column.

A touch on his arm caused him to turn. At his side stood a handsome brunette in willow-green silk. Widowed in her twenties, Margaret Court had taken him to her bed briefly at the end of her year of mourning. Her indiscretion, and their affair had been indiscreet, had freed her, she claimed, from the importunities of men she found priggish and mercenary. She had since married the Earl of Wilton, a man Warne had known at Oxford.

Briefly Margaret's green eyes met his, and both looked away.

"That's a comfort," she said after a pause. "I thought when I saw you here moving about among the nursery set that the fire had gone out."

Warne laughed. "It might among the nursery set," he admitted.

"Well then," she said, "you mustn't linger there."

"But I must if I am to find a wife," he told her.

Her smile did not dim except in those green eyes, which turned from a fiery emerald to a cooler jade. Someone near them gasped, and Warne turned a cold gaze on a handsome blonde in a feathered peach toque. The woman's mouth had dropped open in a little circle of astonishment, but she quickly recovered her composure and moved away.

"Oh dear," said the countess, with a delicate undulation of her ivory fan. "Lady Lacy. You did want your matrimonial ambitions generally known I hope, Warne?"

"I won't need to advertise?" he asked lightly.

"Consider it done," said the countess. "But seriously, Warne, *you* marry?"

"It's time." The irony was that he had felt himself married for years, had considered each brief affair a breach of faith, and only now considered himself free.

"Then what am I to make of the roses that came this morning?" Margaret asked quietly.

Warne tensed and turned to her. "My card was with these roses?"

"Yes, and the—"

"—strangest message," he finished.

"You did not send them I take it?"

"No." He took a deep breath. "Margaret, I am sorry if you were . . . inconvenienced by their arrival."

She waved her hand, dismissing any awkwardness at receiving a floral tribute from her former lover. "They were delivered by a young gentleman this morning," she told him. "Apparently the florist's boy."

"Which florist?" Warne asked, conscious of a slight edge to his voice. He did not wish Margaret embarrassed now by a scandal nearly five years old. She did not know the florist, but she promised to find out and send word to him. With that Warne had to be satisfied, but he felt certain he was going to need a long, long run in the morning to keep his temper in check.

He left the duchess's ball puzzled. His affairs with Diana Ferris and Margaret Court had lasted no more than a few heated weeks, and while he had made no effort to conceal them, they were old scandals now. Yet someone had remembered and chosen to remind his former lovers of their connection with him. He could not think why.

He had set out to find a bride, and now it appeared that he must find a thief.

4

At Lady Lacy's Duke Street residence, Juliet dashed ahead of Susannah and rang the bell with insistent vigor. Her efforts produced a small, white-haired butler, with a goat-like beard, whose cravat was decidedly askew. Juliet brushed past him, leaving the man tottering and gripping the doorknob to retain his balance.

An instant later a decidedly unladylike shriek rent the air, and Juliet reappeared in the doorway holding aloft the highwayman's card.

"He's . . . . He must be an earl. His father's a marquess," she shouted.

Susannah turned to Tim Dachet with instructions about the luggage. Silently she cursed the young highwayman, whom she suspected of reading Minerva Press novels. *An earl? More likely an understudy in a melodrama.*

"Here now, Miss," said the little butler to Juliet. He was holding his head with both hands as if in pain. "Who are you to come bursting in at her ladyship's door, shouting so a man's head would split?"

Juliet drew herself up with haughty dignity. "Who are you?" she demanded. "Where is my mama?"

"I'm Chettle, Miss," said the little man. He peered more closely at Juliet. "Your mama's out."

31

"Out? She can't be out. She knows we arrive tonight." Juliet gave Susannah a puzzled look.

Susannah came up the steps and put out a hand to calm Juliet. "Mr. Chettle, no doubt her ladyship made arrangements for Miss Lacy's arrival," she said quietly.

Under her gaze the little butler straightened his shoulders. Then a second carriage drew up. Chettle muttered a *pardon me* and, abandoning them, descended to aid the new arrival, leaving in his wake the unmistakable odor of spirits. From the second carriage Lady Lacy alighted. She accepted her butler's unsteady arm and began speaking to him at once in low, quick tones.

"That's my mother?" Juliet whispered with a trace of wonder.

Susannah nodded. Evelina Lacy had changed little in ten years. Tall and golden-haired with beautiful blue eyes and a generous bosom, she looked little older than her daughter except for a softness under the chin. And she dressed with a degree of elegance Susannah had never seen in Berkshire. This night Evelina was attired in peach and cream from the feathers on her toque to the slippers on her feet.

When she saw Juliet, she stopped speaking and shook off Chettle's arm. "Juliet, dearest. Is it really you? My little girl?"

"Mama?" Juliet stood still. Whatever memories she had of her mother, she was clearly adjusting her thinking to the elegant reality before her.

Evelina came forward with a rustle of silk and touched her cheek to Juliet's. "How pretty you are!"

She stepped back, and mother and daughter regarded each other silently. With an awkward little laugh, Evelina spoke again. "I hope you don't mind me being out when you arrived. I never miss the duchess of Somerset's ball."

"We only just came, Mama," said Juliet.

Evelina tugged at her long kid gloves and gave Susannah an assessing glance.

"Mama, this is cousin Susannah. Mrs. Bowen, that is," said Juliet.

"Ah, Richard's daughter. Lacy mentioned you, didn't he? Widowed?"

Susannah nodded, and a crashing thump behind them punctuated her unspoken lie. The three ladies turned to find Tim Dachet standing sullenly over Juliet's trunk.

"Chettle," said her ladyship, assuming a sudden command. "See to your duties, and ring Mrs. Chettle for me, please."

Mr. Chettle wobbled off, and his wife appeared in his stead. A stern-faced matron in stiff black skirts, she orderd the footmen about with surprising authority and settled the ladies before a warm fire in an elaborate parlor.

As they sipped tea, Evelina studied her daughter frankly and proclaimed her delight with Juliet's beauty. "How fortunate that you favor me and not your father. We will have no trouble finding you a splendid husband. Why, only tonight there were dozens of eligibles at the Duchess's ball. I must tell you all about it."

Susannah observed her aunt as she spoke. Evelina, it was plain, liked everything that her husband did not—warmth, comfort, extravagance, fashion, and talk. Susannah recalled that her aunt came from a large family, and that before her marriage Evelina had enjoyed all the popularity that prettiness and a substantial dowry could secure. She had not been happy in her marriage, and in the very season that had been so disastrous for Susannah, Evelina and Uncle John had agreed to live in separate residences—hers in town , his in the country. She had surrendered her children to her husband's care.

Juliet, too, watched her mother closely and took in her mother's description of the ball with obvious interest, but she had hardly forgotten their encounter with the highwayman. She turned the small white card over and over between her fingers.

At one of Evelina's pauses, Juliet said, "Now, Mama, you must hear our adventure. We met the most dashing highwayman." In a few breathless sentences she recounted the episode. "And it's all a disguise because he gave me his card, and he's the son of a peer."

"What?" said Evelina. "A titled highwayman?"

"Well, look at the card, Mama." Juliet held out the card and Evelina reached for a pair of reading spectacles.

"Francis William Arden, Marquess of Warne," she read. "Warne? You cannot have met Warne for I saw him tonight at the ball, and heard the most intriguing *on dit*—"

"Not the marquess, Mama," interrupted Juliet. "Our highwayman was quite a young man. You must read the handwritten note."

"'With my father's compliments'," she read. "Well, what does that mean?"

"It means," said Juliet patiently, "that the highwayman is Lord Warne's son. It is romantic beyond anything. I wonder why he must go in disguise holding up coaches on the heath?"

Susannah thought the name Warne familiar and tried to recall where she might have heard it. If the highwayman was truly a young lord, perhaps he had been acting on a wager. She accepted the card Juliet now thrust in her hands. Its message was written in a neat schoolboy hand by someone who had mended his pen well.

A new thought occurred to Susannah.

"You know, Juliet, a marquess or any father may have several sons, and, of course, all cannot inherit equal wealth. Perhaps our highwayman is a younger son."

"But, my dears," said Lady Lacy. "Lord Warne is not married. He has no sons at all."

Susannah and Juliet both stared.

"But he must have, Mama. Our highwayman was a gentleman."

Evelina shook her head. "I'm sure he's no connection of Warne's."

"Perhaps an impostor, acting on a wager," Susannah suggested.

Juliet turned on her. "Susannah, you do spoil everything. He must be Lord Warne's son. He had his card."

"If your mother is right, he can be neither Lord Warne's son, nor a gentleman," Susannah countered. "And you are not likely to see him in town." She knew Juliet was thinking the young man would find them. Confound him for being mysterious. Nothing could be more appealing to one of Juliet's temperament.

"Well, I will look for him. You have no sense of romance, Susannah. In some ballroom he will find me."

"It might be wise to listen to Susannah, Juliet dear," said Evelina. For the first time she looked uneasy about their story. "You must not offend Lord Warne. He's a dangerous man, quite implacable. You know he's called the Iron Lord. He drove his father to an untimely death."

"How?" asked Juliet.

"Well, I hardly know the details. Warne has avoided the *ton* for years, but he is utterly merciless. He bought up his father's vowels and gave them to the moneylenders. The older marquess was quite unwell and in no shape to flee. It ruined dozens of families when the old man went bankrupt."

Again Evelina cast a speculative glance at Susannah. "Wasn't your father one of the men who was ruined when old Warne's West Indies bank failed?"

Susannah flushed. She had heard little of her family after they cast her off. "Yes, I think so." Uncle John must have mentioned Warne in connection with her family's ruin and her parents' death in a carriage accident.

"Still," Evelina pointed out, "Warne is rich as Croesus, and tonight I heard him say that he will choose a bride this season. It could be you, Juliet dear. Imagine a daughter of mine a marchioness and rich as an empress."

"Oh, I'd never want to meet someone that old," said Juliet.

"Old?" said Evelina. She straightened her chin, pressing her hand up against its softness, and Susannah suggested a new topic, diverting her aunt's attention to Juliet's well-cut wool gown.

"Did Lacy give you enough for your clothes, dear?" Evelina asked. "We should see a modiste tomorrow."

Later, by the fire in the comfortable room that had been assigned to her, Susannah took stock of the day. She stretched her toes toward the coals. If the highwayman did not seek Juliet out, if Evelina did indeed know some acceptable gentlemen, and if no word of their adventure came to the ears of the implacable Lord Warne, Juliet might marry wisely yet.

Susannah thought of her uncle's list of suitors. Lord Warne's name was not there though he had greater rank and wealth than any gentleman on the list. Apparently, Uncle John had remembered what Warne had done to Richard and the others. A dangerous man her aunt had said, a man who terrified the *ton* and yet meant to pick a bride from among them. Susannah suddenly pictured a sneering dandy moving down a line of white-gowned misses shaking his head. Did the man think choosing a bride was like . . . choosing a hat?

5

Kirby switched the valise from his right to his left hand and let himself into the lodging house. Though it was well after midnight, lights were burning in several rooms. The residents were theatre people who hardly kept shopkeepers' hours. He made his way up the open oak stair, a relic of an earlier era of elegance, past number one where Draycot, the actor, was obviously entertaining a large party, past number two, where the sounds suggested a more intimate gathering, and up to the landing he shared with Mrs. Hayter. Light seeped from under her door, and he prepared himself for the likelihood that she would call to him. It was through her kindness that he'd got the room.

They had met at the theatre, where she was one of the backers of the company. And without asking what his other business in London was, she had helped him find the masks, wigs, and cosmetics he needed to put his plan into action. No, she would not scold or nag him; she would probably want to be sure that he'd had something to eat. He *had* eaten at Staines, hours ago, but now his stomach grumbled at the thought of food.

Until this very moment he had forgotten. Tonight he'd felt that rush in his veins like one felt at the opening of a play. He had delivered the first two cards, and soon word would get to Warne. The plan was going to work.

And the plan had led him to Juliet Lacy. He had seen her at the edge of the crowd at Staines, seen the bright curiosity with which she looked about her, her eagerness for life and adventure, and her dismay at being restrained by her strict companion. On the spot he decided that she would be the next recipient of a card and had followed them out of Staines, waiting for the opportunity to hold up their coach.

The other robbers had never been part of the plan, but the thrill of thwarting them, of rescuing Miss Lacy and giving her cause to think well of him went beyond anything he had anticipated. He wanted to be alone with it.

Mrs. Hayter's door opened.

"Mr. Kirby," she whispered. "We have not seen you all day. You must be needing a bite to eat."

Kirby faced his own door. His stomach growled again, not a polite anticipatory note, but a full rolling rumble. He thought of Odysseus in the hall of King Alkinoos. "Belly must be filled," the hero had said. Kirby laughed and turned to face his neighbor.

She stood in the entrance to her suite looking quite unlike her daytime self. Her deep red hair, usually elaborately curled, was pulled back in a loose braid under a lacy cap. A jade silk wrapper heightened the white of her skin, and her gray eyes sparkled with tears. For a moment he simply stared. Though he knew her to be close to his mother's age, she looked young and hurt, and the heroic impulse that had come to life in him earlier made him step forward. "Mrs. Hayter, what is it?"

"Oh dear," she said. "You must not note these tears. It's . . . it's just a novel I've been reading. Do come in, Mr. Kirby." She brushed her cheeks with the back of a small white hand and stepped aside, pulling the door open for him.

Kirby entered her apartments, set his valise on the floor, and shed his greatcoat. Mrs. Hayter's two little maids came forward to take the coat, and his hostess led him to a seat in her sitting room, a room furnished with the opulent remains of a more splendid time in her life. Kirby thought about her tear-brightened eyes.

A maid brought a tray with a supper of claret, bread, and cold meat pie, just as if he'd been expected. When they were alone on a gold damask sofa, he turned to Mrs. Hayter. "You've not been reading in here," he said. "The light's too dim. Can't you tell me what's wrong?"

She shook her head. "First, you must eat." She poured some claret and put the glass in his hand. To please her he drank a long swallow of the wine and ate a few bites of the meat pie.

She sat at the other end of the low backless sofa with her feet tucked under her, toying with the end of her braid, watching him politely. At last she began, "You will think me very foolish, Mr. Kirby—"

"Kirby," he corrected her. "It's my given name." In truth it was his mother's name, but as all *his* names were his father's, too, he refused to use them.

"Kirby, then," Mrs. Hayter said. She straightened a little and adjusted the tie of her wrapper under her breasts. White, full breasts, Kirby noted. He took another swallow of wine and felt it loosen his limbs.

"How very unconventional," she said. "I like
that."

"So you will tell me what's troubling you?" he
asked.

She nodded. Tears welled up in her eyes, and she
groped for the pocket of her dressing gown. Kirby
put down the wine glass, scooted across the space
that separated them, and offered his handkerchief,
which she accepted with a tremulous smile, pressing the linen to her eyes.

"Do you ever miss your parents?" she asked, her
wet gray gaze catching his.

He straightened abruptly and looked away. Mrs.
Hayter had spoken of Warne as if she knew of him,
and no one must guess his connection with the peer
before his plan had time to work.

"My mother," he said.

"She must miss you and worry to think of you in
this wicked city alone." Mrs. Hayter reached out
and gave his hand a gentle squeeze.

"She's dead."

His companion gave a little gasp, and the hand
holding his tightened. "I'm so sorry," she said. "I
did not mean to grieve you."

"It's been three years," Kirby replied. "I can speak
of her."

"Tell me," his companion invited. She pulled his
hands into her lap and held them between her own.

Kirby thought fleetingly that it had been his intention to comfort her, but it would be a pleasure to tell
someone about his mother, and Mrs. Hayter was
looking at him with such sympathy and interest
in her shining gray eyes.

So he told her about Ellen Kirby, the vicar's
daughter, the scholar, about her love of Homer and Shakespeare, about her quick laughter,

her determination to provide for him, and her years of humiliation at the hands of cloddish employers.

"She was widowed young, your mother?"

Kirby nodded, letting the lie stand.

"So you did not know your father?" Mrs. Hayter looked at his hands, which she stroked lightly with her own. "But your mother told you of him, how fine he was and how much like him you are?"

Kirby looked sharply at her, but her head remained bent over their hands. He supposed it was a guess. Any mother would tell her son that about an absent father. Hadn't Penelope told Telemakhos how like he was to the missing Odysseus?

But Ellen Kirby had said nothing of her husband until she lay dying. Then she had shown her son clippings and letters, a history of his father's life. Her Odysseus, she called him. She made her son promise that he would present himself to his father in London. Well, Kirby had made the promise, and he would keep it, but in his own way. He wanted nothing from the highborn lord who had abandoned them to live in luxury and sin, indifferent to his wife's suffering, his son's powerlessness—except revenge. He would leave a trail of cards, exposing every episode of his father's infamous conduct.

"I am not at all like him," he told Mrs. Hayter.

At that she raised her glistening gray eyes to his and lifted her soft white hand to his face. With one finger she traced the sharp peak of a brow and the narrow blade of his nose, and touched the corner of his mouth.

Looking down at her, Kirby could see the tops of her breasts, white against the green silk, like foam against the sea, and he had the oddest feeling that she wanted him to pull the dangling ribbon that held her wrapper in place, to spill the soft white flesh into his hands.

His pulse pounded and his male flesh rose. She had withdrawn her hands from his, and his were lying in her lap. He stood abruptly and realized that even in the dim light she could not mistake the state he was in. He had meant to offer comfort and was about to offer insult.

Her head was bowed again as if to spare him any embarrassment.

"I beg your pardon," he whispered, and turned and fled.

As soon as the door closed behind her guest, Molly Hayter rose and took a candle into the little vestibule and knelt beside the valise her maids had moved to one side. With swift, silent efficiency she explored its contents. There was nothing there to surprise her except a bit of brown paper wrapped around some cards. She opened the little package and removed one of the cards.

"What a very poor liar you are, my friend Kirby," she said. "I knew you for his son the minute I saw you." She restored the remaining cards to their package and the contents of the valise to good order and strolled back to her sitting room.

She stopped before the large gilt mirror that dominated the wall above the mantel and gave a little tug on the ribbon that secured her wrapper. The silk slipped away, revealing full white breasts with rosy peaks. Molly studied them dispassionately. She turned the small white card over and looked at it again.

"So you mean to pay your father back, young Arden. Well, I can help you, truly, I can."

6

Evelina insisted on a full round of social engagements for their first day in town, including an appearance in the park at the fashionable hour. Talk had filled the day, idle malice masquerading as solicitude, and Susannah welcomed the clop of hooves and the rumble of carriage wheels that accompanied their progress through the park.

Somewhere between Lady Banks's and Miss Elphinestone's she had developed the tiniest bit of sympathy for Uncle John. Whatever Evelina heard in one drawing room she was sure to repeat in the next. Susannah only hoped her aunt had not made any indiscreet revelations about Juliet's encounter with the young highwayman. Any coupling of Juliet's name with Lord Warne's in an *on dit* was sure to reach the ears of the Iron Lord. And all the gossips agreed he was a dangerous man to offend.

Still Susannah thought they had done well for their first day. If Juliet seemed incapable of forgetting the stranger, she would soon meet eligible gentlemen whose air and manner were certain to impress a girl making her come-out. This happy thought lasted until the driver brought the landau to a stop abreast of another carriage so that Evelina could speak with her particular friend, Mrs. Trentfield.

Susannah recognized her at once. Widowed now, Ann Trentfield had made her come-out with Susannah, and the sharp glance Susannah received from her seemed to say that she remembered something of that other season. Susannah lowered her gaze. She had thought her ruin so old and so insignificant a scandal that no one would recall it. Now she realized she would have to practice all the lessons in humility that she had learned in Uncle John's house. She kept her hands folded in her lap and smiled with polite interest as Evelina repeated an anecdote about Byron she had told a score of times already.

But Susannah's rebellious spirit soon stirred, and she turned away from the talk. The rain of the day before had passed, and the sky was blue with light clouds in high thin lines like the furrows of a new-planted field. The paths invited walking, and she vowed to escape to the park for an early morning ramble. For the moment, however, she must be content to sit quietly and let the wind blow her aunt's voice away. The breeze tugged at her bonnet, and she touched the ribbons to check that they were securely tied.

Juliet, too, was ignoring her mother's conversation, her eyes glancing at gentlemen of a certain height in the passing throng. "I don't care what you think, Susannah," she whispered. "We are in his debt, and I will acknowledge him wherever we meet."

"In that case," Susannah replied, "I hope he has the prudence not to appear in town."

Juliet made a face. "Mama says I needn't fear to speak to whom I please," Juliet asserted. Unspoken was Juliet's awareness of her own beauty. In a blue spencer over white muslin and with a bonnet trimmed in white roses, Miss Lacy looked as fresh and appealing as the March sky above them.

Susannah bit back an intemperate reply and lifted her gaze. Tall elms rose above them with puffs of pale green buds. For a moment, Susannah allowed herself to think of the cottage in Wincanton that would be hers if she could keep Juliet from imprudence. But that pleasant vision of freedom faded when Mrs. Trentfield's tone suggested a confidence of a particularly sensitive nature was about to be revealed.

"Is it true, dear, that your daughter has met Warne's *natural* son?" Ann asked. "A highwayman, is he?"

Susannah gasped. Evelina cast her a quick sheepish glance. They had not called upon Mrs. Trentfield earlier, but evidently she had heard the story, which meant that Evelina *had* been telling it. Dozens of people might have heard it by now, even the haughty Lord Warne himself. And, of course, the truth had been distorted already.

"Really," Evelina protested, "we have no idea who the man is, though he claimed a connection with Warne. My daughter . . ."

At that moment a gust of wind hit them and lifted Juliet's bonnet from her head, wafting it over the horses' backs to the grass beyond and sending it tumbling across the green expanse. Instantly Juliet swung open the carriage door, let down the steps, and descended.

"Juliet," Susannah cried, but her words were snatched away by the breeze as Juliet charged headlong in pursuit of the tumbling bonnet.

Susannah rose and stepped down to follow her cousin. As she touched the ground, she felt herself under scrutiny and looked up. A tall gentleman in a blue coat and buff inexpressibles was watching the little episode. The intensity of the gentleman's gaze made her pause and check a defiant impulse to release her anger. His eyes were as cold as the wind.

At Maria Sefton's urging, Warne joined the *beau monde* for the afternoon ritual of passing one another in the park. Lady Sefton assured him that the park was the place to impress young ladies with his interest or lack of it. And besides she had said, "Your figure shows to advantage on a horse, Warne." She was teasing him, of course, but she knew the ways of the *ton*, and he would do well to heed her advice. At the Somerset ball he had realized how hard it was going to be to overcome the *ton's* distrust of him. He wondered if he had the patience for it. He was used to spending his afternoons pushing himself to accomplish some necessary work for one of the businesses he and Bellaby ran, and he found this amble through the park as tedious as a minuet on horseback.

"That *was* Warne, was it not?" he heard one gentleman say to another as they passed.

He was relieved to encounter the countess of Wilton with her husband. There could be no scandal in his greeting his friends together as a couple.

Lord Wilton introduced the topic of the Lavalette affair, and Warne agreed that the French were a damned unforgiving lot. He glanced at Margaret and found her watching him.

He had received a note from her about the delivery of roses with his card, and he had interviewed the florist. Apparently, a young gentleman had made the purchases and taken the flowers with him. The florist could not say whether the man was fair or dark, well heeled or shabby, but he did recall that the lad had a touch of a Scot accent. The fellow was not one of his father's men then, but a hireling.

"You are the subject of the latest *on dit*, Warne," Margaret told him.

His hands clenched, and his mount danced uneasily. He checked the animal. "With my search for a bride?" he asked.

"That, too," said Margaret, a hint of laughter in her green eyes. Then she sobered. "There is a story going about that a highwayman held up two young ladies of fashion and left them with one of your cards. You know the message it bore. The speculation, of course, is that you have a natural son."

Warne straightened, momentarily forgetting his surroundings. It was too like an exploit of his. He had held up his father's mistress once, relieved her of a necklace his father had given her, and sent the bauble to his mother with his father's compliments. Who but his father would remember and avenge that act? "Who's telling this tale?" he asked.

"Lady Lacy," said Margaret. "The blonde you startled at the Somerset ball."

"Flows as steady as the Thames," said Lord Wilton. He made a gesture with his hand to indicate a mouth opening and closing.

"Her daughter and niece met the man, who handed them your card," Margaret added.

"What did he take from them?" he asked curtly.

"Nothing, that I've heard of."

"Who are they?" He had to know.

"The baron is a miser, I think, keeps to his estate, never comes to town. His lady delights in gossip. I can point her out." Margaret lifted her chin and surveyed the park. "There, in the black landau."

Warne turned to see an odd tableau—the fair but
full beauty he remembered from the Somerset ball,
frozen in mid-speech, a lovely younger version of
the woman tumbling out of the carriage, and a slim
woman in a dark brown cape, leaning out after her.
The fair-haired girl, her golden curls shining in the
afternoon sun, moved as if quite conscious of the
pretty picture she made.

The woman in brown now descended from the
carriage, as lightly as had the other, but with more
dignity. She glanced at him briefly, as if aware of
his scrutiny, and paused, catching his gaze on her.
A defiant spark flashed in the dark eyes and was
instantly veiled. Warne thought it a trick of habit.
He had a moment to note the straight, slim figure
in the brown cape. Then with a quick, purposeful
stride the woman set off after the girl chasing the
bonnet.

Warne was sure they had no connection with
him, had never been part of his life, yet the fellow with the cards, the man who seemed to know
Warne's past, had given them his card. It made no
sense, and it certainly was nothing his father would
have planned. But they had met his thief and would
know whether he was young or old, tall or short, fat
or lean, well-bred or an oaf. So Warne must meet
them.

Kirby leaned upon the cane he had borrowed
from Draycot. He felt he had the hang of it now,
and tapped along the path quite confidently. He had
had another success. He had managed to purchase a
fine new beaver on the strength of his father's card,
and he had come to the park to seek his father out
and tip the new hat to him. For once Lord Warne was
providing for the son he'd fathered and forgotten.

The only difficult moment in the whole scheme had come when the haberdasher, looking up from the card, had addressed Kirby as "my lord." He had been obliged to drop one of his packages in order to conceal his surprise. He realized then that he had not been clear-headed about the long list of Warne's titles. The entry in *Debrett's* applied to his grandfather, and he had not considered that now that his father had inherited, Dovedale would be his son's title, if that son were acknowledged.

It was that realization as much as anything that had drawn him to the park to look upon the *ton*. He had donned a gray wig and beard and now leaned upon a cane, but he wore the curly brimmed beaver he had purchased at a jaunty angle. He was or should be one of them, one of these idlers, at leisure to drive or stroll through the park, admiring each other in clothes they would soon change for their evening attire while lesser mortals sewed and pressed and fetched and cleaned to keep them in style.

He told himself he was not seeking Juliet Lacy. His embarrassing encounter with Mrs. Hayter had recalled him to his purpose. He had no business pursuing a girl no matter how fresh and lovely she seemed, no matter her courage and eagerness for life. He would fulfill his promise to his mother, and his own plans for his father's humiliation, and leave London. Falling in love had no part in his plans. Still he found himself searching for that one face in the crowd, and when he found it, he could not help fixing his gaze there.

She, too, was looking at passing faces. He could see how little attention she gave to her companions. The woman in the brown cape must be her

sensible cousin from the night before. And there
was no mistaking the other woman. She could be
none other than Juliet's mother. He passed them
once, then turned and doubled back, passing again,
inches from Miss Lacy. Another turn and he was
facing them once again, moving as slowly as he
dared, prolonging the occasion. Then fortune favored him. The wind lifted Miss Lacy's bonnet and
sent it scudding across the grass. The young lady
herself descended from the carriage with the same
impulsive quickness he had seen the night before.
Kirby was already in motion. The wind was blowing the bonnet his way, and he had only to step off
the path a few paces and wait for the breeze to
bring it to him. A playful gust dropped it within
reach, and Kirby planted his cane upon the ribbons.

The girl came to a breathless halt before him.
"My bonnet, please, sir," she said, her eyes on the
object in question.

"May I ask a *boon* of you then, Miss Lacy?" he
answered.

Her head came up abruptly, and her startled eyes
sought his.

"You?" She was studying him, trying to penetrate the wig and beard.

"At your service," he said with a slight bow. He
bent down to retrieve the bonnet.

"Why are you are in disguise?" she asked. "Are
you in danger?"

He nodded, holding out the bonnet.

"Then you can't come to call?"

He shook his head. Speaking slowly, he told her,
"You must not let anyone know you've seen me in
London."

"Are you really Lord Warne's son?"

"I must go, Miss Lacy. Your cousin approaches. Tell no one we met here."

She looked so downcast at this ending of their conversation that he added, "Do you ever go to Lackington's?"

"No."

He turned away.

"But I will," she called, and the wind carried her voice to him.

When he was safely hidden in the crowd again, he turned back to see her mother's footman helping her into the carriage. Beyond her on horseback, studying the scene, was his father. At the sight, Kirby's hand did shake upon his cane, as if he were indeed the palsied old man he'd pretended to be. His father, titled, wealthy, and free, could court any young lady in London, and it was plain Miss Lacy was here for the season.

7

Susannah wore her lace cap to Lady Shalford's ball, and when their hostess greeted them with a cold, tight smile, Evelina frowned. On the threshold of the ballroom she paused to whisper, "It's your cap, Susannah. I begged you not to wear such an article to a ball. You have no sense of fashion, dear."

Susannah's fingers clenched around her fan. Below them, the *ton*, formidable in its careless elegance, glittered and shimmered in the radiance of a thousand candles. How had she dared to come among them again? Beside her Juliet let out her breath in an exclamation of unabashed delight.

"There's Esther," said Evelina. "Come girls." She led them into the crowd, apparently unconcerned by the curious stares that followed them.

Susannah and Juliet trailed after her, Juliet's eyes searching the crowd. "Do you think he's here?"

Susannah shook her head. "It's doubtful," she said mildly. "Young men have endless resources for entertainment in town, and you can hardly expect your highwayman to attend anything so tame as a ball."

"He must be here," Juliet insisted.

"Not after you've made him notorious with your story of meeting him," Susannah pointed out.

At that, Juliet stopped glancing about. She looked a bit stung, but recovered at once. "I hardly told anyone, just Mama and Mrs. Garthe, and besides he could come . . . in disguise," she said, resuming her search.

Susannah decided the tale of their encounter with the highwayman must be in wide circulation. No one gave them the cut direct, but no one greeted them either. The eyes of the gentlemen did tend to linger on Juliet, a white satin gown on her striking form, a crown of white roses in her golden hair.

Esther Pemford, Evelina's sister, met them before they had advanced very far into the room. Tall, elegant, Titian-haired, with a dark, haughty gaze, she planted herself squarely in their path.

"Evelina, dear," said Mrs. Pemford. "You've done it this time." She nodded to Susannah and shook her head, looking at Juliet. "And such a pretty child."

"Done what?" asked Evelina, her gloved fingers making delicate adjustments to the curls at the side of her face.

"Why chattered too much, of course."

Evelina opened her mouth to protest, but the other woman cut her off with a snap of her fan.

"It's no use, Evie. Look about you. By now everyone's heard that your lovely daughter received Warne's card from a highwayman. What were you thinking to allow such a tale to get about?"

"What's the harm in it? Surely my Juliet did no wrong."

"No? She's landed in the middle of a bumble broth. Whoever this fellow with the card was, he can't be a friend of Warne's. Evie, you do not want an enemy in Warne. And, as you can see, nor does anyone else."

"But what are we to do? The tale's out."

"Put a bold front on it. Stick to the family. Cousin Clara is here. She can introduce the girl to Brentwood. Everyone else will wait to see what Warne does, I expect."

"Warne comes here tonight?" Evelina's gaze again swept the ballroom.

"Don't be a goose, Evie. Of course he does, he's looking for a wife, isn't he? Not that it will be easy for him with his reputation. Even if Maria Sefton is sponsoring him."

"Maria Sefton?" asked Evelina faintly. "I was counting on her for vouchers."

"The more fool, you, Evie. Though I think Maria will have better luck with Warne than she's had with Byron," she added.

"Is Lord Byron here?" asked Juliet.

"I should hope not," said Mrs. Pemford, giving Juliet a quelling glance. "The state that man's affairs are in. Come, ladies."

She led them to a diminutive brunette with a loud ready laugh and constant toothy grin. Cousin Clara dismissed their difficulty with the reflection that, "No one's above the taint of gossip. Lord, not even Wellington, and the entire country's in his debt."

Having made this assurance, Cousin Clara promptly abandoned them to pursue a flirtation of her own, and for several sets, Juliet and Susannah were obliged to stand by while other girls danced, and Evelina pointed out her particular friends, lamenting their inattention to her plight.

Juliet complained of the heat and glitter, the din, and the warm confusion of powerful scents. Her shoulders sagged, and her smile faded.

Susannah said what she could to keep Juliet's spirits up, but she, too, found watching the danc-

ing unbearable. The only music in Uncle John's
house had been Juliet's earnest renderings of familiar ballads on the pianoforte, nothing to stir the
spirit or urge the feet to move. How had Susannah
imagined she could endure a ball? She who had
always been complimented on her dancing. Even
her seducer had praised her light feet and easy
movement, but for ten years her steps had been
no more than tiny, even stitches across a tight frame
of duty and penance. Only her walks had freed her
to move unconstrainedly, and she had not walked
for days.

As a third set formed, Juliet turned to Susannah.
"He's not here, and I am never to meet anyone. This
is too humiliating. I want to go home."

Just then the flirtatious Clara found a moment to
present them to Lord Brentwood, who would take
them in to supper. A viscount in his early thirties,
Brentwood was one of the three men Uncle John
considered most eligible for Juliet's hand. Brentwood was a handsome, solid-looking gentleman,
a little ponderous in his speech, and undoubtedly
aware of the attractions of his rank and purse.

He seemed indifferent to the undercurrents of
gossip and doubt swirling about them. He smiled
at Juliet at once and pronounced what he apparently considered must be her sentiments. "Miss Lacy,
I daresay you find yourself impressed with your
first London ball. Don't find such society in Berkshire, do you?" He looked about the ballroom as if
admiring his own splendid domain.

"There are not so many people at a country ball,
to be sure, my lord," Juliet answered.

"No, of course not," his lordship replied. He went
on to explain in considerable detail the distribution
of the population as reported in the most recent cen-

sus. His hands moved expressively as he talked, and he gave the least question a full answer.

Indeed, at the supper interval, Lord Brentwood only interrupted his population treatise just long enough to offer his arm to Evelina. His gaze remained on Juliet. "Daresay there's five hundred in this room alone. Shalford always draws a crush. French cook, you know. Prinny..." He paused to let the name sink in. "... tried to hire the man away. Couldn't."

They advanced with the crowd in little shuffling steps that reminded Susannah of sheep passing through a narrow gate. The press squeezed them into another long high-ceilinged room, where a generous buffet drew most of the guests. Lord Brentwood steered them toward a cluster of little tables and gilt-edged chairs.

"Does a cook make such a difference at a ball?" Juliet asked Brentwood as he drew out one of the elegant little chairs to seat Evelina.

It was then that the gentleman from the park entered the supper room. Susannah felt the change in mood immediately and turned. He seemed to be looking straight at her, and then his gaze shifted to Juliet. Around them a hundred conversations hushed, suspended by the talkers' awareness that some curious drama was about to be played out before their eyes, and Susannah understood that the gentleman must be Lord Warne.

Warne was not such a stranger to the ballrooms of the *ton* that he did not recognize the avid if veiled attention his arrival received.

Maria Sefton came up to him at once and whispered in his ear, "You've heard, of course."

He nodded.

"Miss Lacy has had a long night, I fear."

"Has she?" He offered his arm to his friend.

"No one wants to incur your displeasure, Warne."

He laughed a short, harsh laugh. "Would that that were a compliment."

His sister's friends were willing enough to welcome him back into society, but for the rest he could imagine their doubts about the Iron Lord.

"They fear you Warne. It's as simple as that. Now, would you care to meet the young lady? You could save her from social ruin and prove that you do not consume young maidens for breakfast." Maria raised one delicate brow.

He laughed. It would suit his purpose to be presented to Miss Lacy. He had given considerable thought to the rumor he'd heard in the park, but try as he might, he could not think of any connection between this green girl and himself. She must have been a mere babe when he began his feud with his father. Her family was unknown to his, he was sure, and even such property as he had in Berkshire was in Wincanton and not near her father's seat at Pangbourne. He'd checked on that. Still there must be some connection, or else he did not understand the card thief at all.

The difficulty was to discover the connection. He could ask the girl about her adventure, but that would be to acknowledge his keen interest in the affair, and put him in a position of dependence upon her honesty and willingness to tell him about the event. She might very well refuse. It seemed a wiser course to ignore the rumors, make the girl's acquaintance, and piece together the details of her adventure from such questions as everyone always asked everyone else about travel.

He studied her as they made their way across

the room. Pretty and conscious of it, she appeared
to be enduring Brentwood's attentions with some
grace. His gaze moved inevitably to her companion, sitting a little apart, as austere as before, her
eyes downcast, her hands resting in her lap, folded
around a fan. He thought her as taut as a bow, and
he did not remember seeing a cap like that since his
last visit to his sister in Bath.

8

Susannah watched Lord Warne's approach. He made way for his companion and himself as if the other guests, whatever their rank and wealth, were as unresisting a medium as air. His indifference to opinion was plain in that unwavering advance, and he was heading for Juliet.

Evelina gave a little moan. "Oh dear, it's Warne."

Brentwood broke off mid-sentence and turned a perplexed gaze on her ladyship. Susannah spoke up then, saying, "Lord Brentwood, what were you saying about the *roulade de boeuf*?"

"Mama," Juliet whispered. "We don't wish to meet Lord Warne, do we?"

"We cannot avoid it. He's with Maria Sefton." Evelina began to wring her hands and look about as if some avenue of escape might present itself.

Brentwood was once more lost in his own eloquence. Susannah smiled and nodded at him, but she felt Warne's approach. It was not what she had expected, and she could not think what he meant by it. He must have heard the gossip, and he could not have liked it. She clutched her fan and felt the ivory sticks bend in her hand. And then he was there, and they were rising, Evelina affecting surprise and pleasure, Lord Brentwood confused.

60

Lady Sefton cast Evelina a calming glance and managed the introductions with creditable tact. Warne she described as a gentleman just returning to society and in need of friends. "I know how well-connected you are, Evelina," she said.

Evelina smiled and nodded and fluttered her fan. Juliet made a scrupulous curtsy, but gave the marquess a frankly curious glance, as if she were looking for some resemblance to the young highwayman. The two men were of equal height, Susannah thought.

She heard herself named Mrs. Bowen, saw Lord Warne note her cap, and had the distinct impression his blue eyes questioned it. Then Maria Sefton drew Evelina aside with the mention of Byron's latest difficulty, and Brentwood cleared his throat.

A frown creased his lordship's smooth forehead. "I was just telling Miss Lacy about Shalford's cook," said Brentwood with mild belligerence.

"I have no objection," said Warne.

Susannah glanced at him. The words were said with no apparent irony, but she had the feeling the marquess had just invited Brentwood to be stupid.

Warne reached for one of the little chairs and drew it near for Juliet, who dropped obediently into the seat. Then he was at Susannah's side offering her a chair. Their eyes met briefly, his unreadable. He seated himself next to her and looked up at Brentwood, who abruptly turned to locate a chair for himself.

"As I was saying," Brentwood began.

When she could, Susannah studied the marquess. What did he mean by securing an introduction to Juliet? His face wore an expression of polite interest, but she was sure the blue eyes missed nothing. He made her decidedly uncomfortable, as if a fox had been invited to a party of ducks and geese.

It was not his appearance that had such an effect. Not his hair, which was brown really, with hints of red and gold, fine and thick like a boy's. Nor the blue eyes, which did not suggest guile so much as clear-headedness and wit. Nor the narrow nose, with its hint of a haughty curve. Nor the mouth, which stretched easily into a grin. Nor the way he disposed himself in the chair, one long, muscled leg stretched out. That muscled leg bothered her, she admitted to herself.

She had quite removed herself from men in her exile. There had been farmers and shepherds and furze cutters on market days, the vicar on Sundays, and Uncle John every day. But none whose manliness intruded on her notice. Even when the vicar had taken a brief fancy to her. He had always reminded her of wet dogs, and she had not been overly disappointed when Uncle John had discouraged the man's suit even though there had followed a series of sermons on the sins of the flesh.

Here in this room with hundreds of men in their finery, Lord Warne's leg was a shock. His voice, when he entered the conversation, was a low rumble at her side, the deep resonance of it unsettling.

"Miss Lacy," he asked Juliet, "are you *very* interested in the domestic arrangements of the *ton*?"

"Oh no," Juliet replied, with what could only be considered heartfelt sincerity.

Lord Brentwood choked, and Susannah came alert.

"Really," Juliet said, "I am more interested in . . ." she glanced at Susannah, and finished, " . . . enjoying the season."

"What is it, then, that you hope to enjoy in town?" the marquess asked.

Juliet looked down and arranged her skirts over her knees. "We only just arrived last night," she said.

"Ah, just arrived," he said. "Then Brentwood and I have been remiss in not asking you about your journey. Did you come post or in your own equipage?"

"Oh, in Papa's carriage, of course," answered Juliet, giving her fan a languid wave.

Susannah cast her charge a warning glance. Juliet seemed to think she could play this game, but the marquess took swift and dangerous control of the conversation and turned it toward his ends.

"You make light of such a journey, Miss Lacy, but did you have postilions and outriders enough for your safety and consequence?" he asked.

"Just Tim Dachet and John Coachman as always," said Juliet with a shrug.

"What do you think, Brentwood?" asked the marquess, turning to the other man. "Was Miss Lacy trusting too much to luck, or are the roads safe enough for young ladies travelling by private carriage with but two guards?"

Lord Brentwood's hands went into motion at once as he informed them of the extent of criminal activity in the environs of London. The marquess studied Juliet, and Susannah had the feeling that no sign of her cousin's uneasiness would escape him. When a gasp from Juliet interrupted Brentwood's account of the bludgeoning of a family of four, Susannah intervened, turning to the marquess and drawing his gaze. "Surely the dangers of travel by private coach have been exaggerated," she said. The keen blue eyes seemed to measure her intent.

"Oh yes," Juliet agreed. "There's hardly enough adventure to suit me. Travelling is mostly tedious, for Coachman will go slowly, and Susannah—"

The mention of her name appeared to distract the marquess briefly, but he turned and asked Juliet, "What, no adventures, Miss Lacy? Surely every heroine deserves one good adventure on the road to London."

"But I am not a heroine, Lord Warne," Juliet replied, plainly perplexed by the suggestion.

"Not fated like your famous namesake to meet some masked Romeo at a ball?" he asked lightly.

"Oh," said Juliet with evident dismay, clearly recognizing the marquess's trap now that it had sprung on her. She fanned her bright cheeks vigorously. "No . . . such thing would ever happen to me, I'm sure."

"Of course not," interrupted Brentwood. "A perfectly respectable ball this, no need to alarm Miss Lacy with fate."

"Yet," said Lord Warne, "I had the distinct impression Miss Lacy did not wish to be . . . dull."

The strains of the orchestra resuming its playing reached them, and Susannah turned to Lord Brentwood, suggesting that what Juliet wished for above all was to be dancing. She smiled at the viscount, who failed to take the hint. He had a point he wished to make about fate.

"You are not engaged for this set, Miss Lacy?" Warne asked, and Juliet admitted she was not. She had only time to cast a quick worried glance at Susannah as the marquess rose and offered his arm. He looked back over his shoulder as if to acknowledge the advantage he had gained, and Susannah frowned at Brentwood.

* * *

Juliet and Lord Warne danced a quadrille of the more intricate variety, which allowed but a few occasions for conversation. Susannah watched those exchanges closely but could detect no signs of displeasure or discovery in the marquess. When the set ended, he returned a thoughtful Juliet to Susannah's side.

"He's not so mean as Mama says," Juliet confided.

"He did not press you any more about your adventure?"

Juliet adjusted the modest neckline of her gown to a more daring degree. "Not at all."

"What *did* you talk about?" Susannah asked. She feared that Lord Warne was quite capable of encouraging Juliet to make indiscreet revelations.

"Just things. Berkshire, Mama, you."

"Me?" Susannah could not prevent the note of surprise in her voice.

"Yes. Lord Warne wanted to know how long you had been a widow. I told him I didn't really know," said Juliet. "Since before you came to us, I suppose." She gave Susannah a sly look.

"Why else would I have come," Susannah said lightly, but she felt a little knot of fear inside. Long ago she had invented the fictional Mr. Bowen, a hero who had died with Sir John Moore at Corruna, but how easily that lie could be exposed.

Juliet regarded her now with frank curiosity, and Susannah strove to compose herself, grateful when Lord Brentwood interrupted their exchange to claim a dance. She had no qualms about her cousin's dancing with the prosy viscount and took one of the seats reserved for chaperones.

At the end of the set, Juliet stepped from Lord Brentwood's side into a circle of gentlemen—Cousin Clara's work—wishing to be presented to her. Clara presided over these introductions, and Susannah could have laughed at such an improvement in Juliet's social position after just two dances, one with Lord Warne. But she was too familiar with society's fickle nature. Juliet could again become the subject of gossip and be shunned. Look at Byron, who had been lionized, and now was universally reviled and Susannah herself, who had been foolish, and condemned for it, and who, with the false name of Bowen, was acceptable again.

When the orchestra took up an entirely new tune, Juliet's admirers asked Susannah if Miss Lacy were permitted to waltz. Susannah shook her head. There was a groan from the young men, but one, perhaps kinder than the rest, offered to sit the dance out to keep Miss Lacy company. His friends accused him of baser motives, and all agreed to stay by Juliet's side.

Susannah found herself squeezed out of the circle, but her seat allowed a clear view of the dancers. She had heard of the waltz, of course. Not long before, the dance had been censured by nearly everyone, including Byron, but Susannah and Juliet had practiced the steps. They had purchased *The Correct Method of German and French Waltzing* by T. Wilson, Dancing Master, King's Theatre. But whirling about with Juliet unaccompanied by any instrument, the waltz seemed no more than a mild exercise, not an intimate union. And Susannah had failed, without hearing the music, to comprehend its seductive power. She could see now that it produced a soaring giddiness more intoxicating than champagne. Even as she sat with her slippers firmly planted on the floor, she could feel the melody tugging at her, lifting her, seducing her from sense and prudence and duty. She clutched her fan tightly with both hands.

"You will break the sticks, Mrs. Bowen," said a voice at her side. She started and lifted her gaze to find the marquess standing at the edge of her chair, studying her intently. He took her hands in his and loosened her grip on the little fan. The manner in which it was done, at once careless and gentle, sent a hot current of sensation through her. When he released her, her hands burned from the contact, and she buried them in her lap.

"You do not dance?" he asked, seating himself beside her.

"Of course not," she replied.

"You have no wish to cut a dash among the ladies of the *ton*?"

Susannah touched one shaky hand to the little lace cap on her head. It was still there. "Cut a dash? Lord Warne, you cannot make me believe you are ignorant of the nuances of ladies' dress. Do you see one woman dancing with a cap such as this? Such as chaperones wear?"

"Not one," he agreed cheerfully. "But I do see Mrs. Trentfield, a widow, whose year of mourning has just this day ended if the gossips may be believed. Your cousin says that you have been a widow for many years."

Susannah lowered her gaze and spoke the familiar lie. "Yes. Bowen has been dead since Corunna."

"Then you wear your cap because you failed to snare another husband in the interval?"

"Snare?" she said, lifting her chin to stare him full in the face, ready to relieve herself of a blistering

condemnation of gentlemen who imagined that all
the treachery of love was on the woman's side.
She saw a teasing gleam in his eyes and knew that
she had fallen into his trap. She shut her mouth
abruptly and lowered her gaze. She had revealed
a weakness to the clever man at her side, and no
doubt he would use it against her.

The lilting music filled a brief pause, but Susannah felt his scrutiny.

"How do you manage it?" he asked.

"What?"

"That trick of lowering your lashes to hide the
fire inside."

Susannah gripped her fan tighter and strove to
recall her purpose. "I am not here to seek dancing
partners or a husband," she told him. "My duty is
to my cousin. Her match is my concern this season."

"Her mama's too, of course," he said, looking
across the room at Evelina engrossed in earnest
conversation with a woman Susannah did not
know. Her aunt appeared to have forgotten Juliet
entirely.

Susannah blushed and straightened. The man
was too shrewd. Either her aunt was irresponsible,
or her own chaperonage of Juliet was redundant
and officious.

"My cousin's parents do not entirely agree on the
most suitable match for her," she said firmly, meeting his gaze with a level look of her own.

"And you are here to represent your uncle's
views?"

"Yes."

"A serious responsibility that allows no time for
dancing?" His gaze shifted to Juliet and the gentlemen surrounding her.

"My lord, I will see my cousin safely wed," she said.

"*Safely*?" With a look of swift comprehension, his eyes returned to Susannah. "Hence Brentwood, Mrs. Bowen?" He shook his head.

Susannah stared at him. "My lord, excuse me. I can't think what you mean," she said.

"But you can, Mrs. Bowen."

"If I do understand you," she said with heat, "you are presuming to suggest that Lord Brentwood is not a proper suitor for my cousin, with whom you have the merest acquaintance. And that is a piece of long-nosed effrontery—"

He laughed, an undeniably pleasant sound. "Long-nosed effrontery? Dance with me, Mrs. Bowen."

"Pray, excuse me, Lord Warne." She rose abruptly, intent on distancing herself from him, but he stood, catching her wrist and holding it so that she was obliged to stand at his side. She looked pointedly at the gloved hand gripping hers. After a moment his hold gentled, and he released her.

"Mrs. Bowen, do not deny that you have been longing to dance this evening."

Susannah stared at him and shook her head. How had he recognized her longing?

"If not to please me, then for your cousin's sake," he said. "To show the world there is no ill will between myself and the Lacys."

There it was, just as she'd suspected. He had been looking for her weakness, hoping that she might be the one to tell him what he wished to know about their adventure. Oh, he was clever. He guessed how susceptible she would be to a little flattery, a little attention, a chaperone in her cap, a widow, no doubt starved for a man's notice. But she had her unruly spirit firmly in hand now.

"I am glad you harbor no resentment against Miss Lacy," she said carefully. "My cousin can hardly be held responsible for the acts of rash young men or for her mother's indiscreet tongue. I promise to do my best to keep her from incurring your displeasure."

The blue eyes narrowed dangerously. He understood her.

She offered him a parting nod and made her way to Juliet's side, smiling at the gentlemen around her cousin. She would see Juliet safely wed no matter what Lord Warne had to say.

9

With a rare burst of sense, Evelina insisted that Juliet not be at home to callers the day following the Shalford ball. She seemed to realize that Juliet had had an unexpected degree of success and argued that her daughter should keep any interested gentlemen waiting. They shopped and made calls and returned to find the basket on the entry table filled with cards.

The Marquess of Warne sent roses for Juliet and violets for Susannah. Juliet pointed out to her mother that the card with the roses was indeed the same card the highwayman had given her, which prompted Evelina to say, "He means to court you, dear. I knew Esther made too much of that episode."

She drifted off to consult Mrs. Chettle, and Juliet turned to Susannah. "I wonder what he means sending *you* flowers, cousin?"

"He means it as a courtesy to you, I imagine," Susannah replied.

"I don't think so." Juliet gave Susannah a curious glance. "He talked more to you than he did to me. I suppose you are more nearly his age."

Susannah did not reply. If Lord Warne meant to weaken her defenses with violets, he was mistaken in her character.

71

* * *

Kirby made three visits to Lackington's in Finsbury Square before he was rewarded by the sight of Miss Lacy among the shoppers. She looked particularly fine in a close-fitting blue jacket and dainty white bonnet. She took no notice of the books, but began at once to look about at the other customers. He had positioned himself in the corner where two rows of scholarly works in Greek were kept, and his prior visits had convinced the clerks that he was an elderly pedant interested in the current debate on Homer's authorship of *The Iliad*. In spite of the itchy discomfort of the false beard and moustache, he had been following Archer's treatise in favor of a single author for the epic.

He had picked Lackington's because the size of the establishment invited wandering and permitted private conversation, but he saw an additional advantage to such a meeting place as Miss Lacy's cousin gazed in wonder at the floor-to-ceiling shelves. A clerk approached the two ladies, and after a short exchange led the cousin to a section Kirby knew to be devoted to modern poets. Miss Lacy trailed behind.

Her cousin accepted a volume from the clerk and on opening the book seemed to forget Juliet, who hesitated less than a minute, then began making her way around the large room, looking closely at the other patrons. He returned his book to the shelf and leaned on his cane, moving with a slow hobble toward the girl. Their paths crossed at one of the tall ladders to the highest shelves. He pulled a volume from the shelf on his side of the ladder and held it out to her, saying, "Excuse me, Miss . . . Lacy, but can you read this title for me? I can't quite make it out without my eyeglasses."

She whirled to face him, and he knew he was smiling idiotically.

"You," she whispered. "I'm so glad. I thought we would never make it here."

"Was it so difficult to manage?"

"You have no idea. Mama and Susannah have insisted on so many calls and errands. And," she confided, "to have pressed Susannah when she knows I am not at all bookish would have made her quite suspect my motives."

"She doesn't suspect?"

Miss Lacy glanced over her shoulder. "Not at all."

"Good," he said.

A clerk approached to move the ladder, and Kirby put aside his book and offered his arm to Miss Lacy. "Come along, miss," he said in an avuncular tone. "Let's find that book you mentioned."

"I looked for you at the Shalfords' ball," she confided when they had passed beyond the clerk.

He stopped and turned so that he could keep an eye upon her cousin on the opposite side of the great circular counter.

"Would you have danced with me?" he asked, drawing another book from the shelves and opening it.

"Of course."

"Though we've not been properly introduced?" He found the title page.

"I suppose you think me overbold or foolish," she said, looking down for the first time in their conversation.

With two gloved fingers he gently lifted her chin. "Nae," he said. "Did you enjoy the ball?"

"I met a great many gentlemen," she told him. "Including Lord Warne." Her eyes searched his face.

"Did you tell him about our meeting?" he asked,

studying the book in his hand as a clerk passed.

"You asked me not to," she said, obviously offended that he would suggest it, but ill at ease and toying with her bonnet strings. After a pause she admitted, "He knows you gave me his card."

"That's good. That's what I wanted him to know."

"Am I never to see you without a disguise?" she asked.

"I don't know," he answered. "Would you mind very much if we know each other just for awhile?"

"You are only amusing yourself with me then," she protested.

"Hardly!" The word came out more strongly than he'd intended. "But I can make no promises to you. I . . . I am like a soldier going off to war. I don't know what may happen to me."

"Will you hold up more coaches?"

"Nae," he said, and laughed when her face fell. "But I plan to do a few things more daring still." He saw the cousin lift her head and look their way. "Take this book," he ordered, pushing the fat volume into her hands. "Start toward your cousin." He stepped back and faced the shelves, allowing himself to watch Miss Lacy with a side glance.

She turned, held up the book, and smiled across the room at the other woman.

"How will I see you again?" she asked, her head slightly tilted his way.

"What are your engagements?" he whispered to her back. "I can find you if I know."

"Tonight, a dinner. Tomorrow, the theatre. Wednesday, Almack's, of course. And Saturday another ball, but I don't know where."

"I'll find you," he told her and began to hobble away without looking back.

"Susannah, look what I've found," he heard her say. *"The Spanish Brothers.* Don't you think that sounds intriguing?"

Lady Lacy's regular at-home day brought two of Uncle John's acceptable suitors to the blue and gold drawing room, but Susannah's efforts to encourage Juliet to notice them failed miserably.

Lord Brentwood called and soon found himself addressing an empty chair. Lord Atwell, a second gentleman from Uncle John's list, presented himself with little more success. A widower with two daughters, and a passion for politics, he was lean with thinning hair, pale blue eyes, and sharp features. Susannah found him intelligent and informative, though she suspected he rather failed to see any point of view but his own. However, she was the only one interested in what Lord Atwell had to say. Juliet appeared not to notice when he left.

Evelina greeted their next callers, three young gentlemen in elegant coats and ear-scraping collars, with more apparent delight, and they settled themselves in blue-cushioned gilt chairs for an extended visit. These were just the sort of young men who must please—handsome, well-born, and fashionable, her aunt confided to Susannah. Juliet cheerfully confused one with the other.

"Mr. Garrett," she asked. "Are you the hunting-mad gentleman, or is that you, Lord Eastham?"

When Eastham acknowledged that he might be described by his passion for the hunt, she smiled at the third gentleman present and said triumphantly, "Then you, Sir Miles, must be the one who told me about his horses."

Sir Miles Newbury nodded. Susannah suppressed a sigh and prayed silently that Juliet's directness would do her no harm in the eyes of her callers. However, when Juliet abruptly abandoned the gentlemen to greet the Phillips twins, two smart brunettes, who arrived with Mrs. Pemford, Susannah's hopes for the morning dimmed. She smiled at the three astonished young men and quietly moved to Juliet's side, suggesting that their new guests might wish to be presented to the gentlemen.

The Phillips twins, when presented, showed a gratifying interest in Juliet's visitors, and Susannah withdrew, picking up an embroidery frame and settling herself in the windowseat in a patch of pale sunlight. Tomorrow she would rise early and walk and clear her head and decide how to encourage Juliet's notice of appropriate young men.

In the center of the young people, Juliet offered her opinion that London was sadly flat, and her companions protested loudly. The squabble reminded Susannah of geese vying for a farmer's wife's attention. It stopped abruptly when Chettle announced the Marquess of Warne. Susannah lifted her head. His glance rested on her briefly before he turned to his hostess.

The blue and gold drawing room was too fussy for Warne's taste, and must explain why his gaze went first to the slim, straight back of Mrs. Bowen. Her gray silk gown had the dull sheen of pewter, and that delicate back moved him more than the round swell of breast displayed by the other ladies present. Her head was bent over some needlework, and the sheer fabric of her cap caught and held the light while the sun picked out fiery gleams in her dark hair. Her hands moved lightly as she set stitches in a frame. He felt he had not *seen* her properly before. She looked up, and with an effort he withdrew his gaze and greeted his hostess. He had come to find out more about Miss Lacy's connection with his card thief.

He allowed his hostess to present him to the other ladies as if he were a prize she'd captured, endured their appraising glances, accepted the lingering touch of several soft hands, and avoided looking again in Mrs. Bowen's direction. If he must play the suitor to Miss Lacy, he would. The talk in the circle around Miss Lacy, and she was the center of it, was all of the delights to be enjoyed in London, yet the young lady seemed unconvinced. She turned to him, asking, "Have you ever done anything truly daring, Lord Warne?"

Like hold up a coach on Hounslow Heath? He held the words back and watched the girl. She colored as with some belated recollection of the unwisdom of putting such a question to him, and looked as if she might willingly unsay it.

"You put me in an awkward position, Miss Lacy," he said. "If I say yes, I appear to be boasting. If I say no, you will condemn me for dullness. Perhaps you should define what you mean by truly daring."

She smiled, too direct to conceal her relief that he had not made more of the opening her question had given him.

"I merely meant the sort of doings one reads of. The Spanish brothers are forever tangling with . . . highwaymen and pirates and fighting desperate battles and rescuing gentlewomen."

"In London?"

"No, of course not. That is my complaint. Such

things are hardly possible in London," she said.

"I suppose the age of highwaymen is over," he agreed. "No Dick Turpins to be hanged at Tyburn any longer."

"Hanged!" she said, rising a little out of her chair and shooting a brief glance at Mrs. Bowen. She lowered her voice. "They hang them? Not if . . . no one is hurt or . . . nothing is taken?"

"I saw a fellow hanged once," said Sir Miles with a slight shudder. "Didn't care for it. Wouldn't go again."

One of the Miss Phillipses pressed Sir Miles, in spite of his obvious repugnance, to tell more about the execution, but Miss Lacy continued to stare at Warne. Her blue eyes suggested that the young lady was doing a great deal of rapid thinking.

"What was the fellow hanged for, Newbury?" asked Eastham as Sir Miles came to the end of his story.

"Don't know," said Sir Miles.

"They shoot traitors now," offered Mr. Garrett. "The French even shot Ney!" He shook his head.

"But Lavalette escaped," Warne added for Miss Lacy's benefit. She looked decidedly pale and strained.

"Disguised himself as an English general, got clean away. Now that's daring for you, isn't it, Miss Lacy?" asked Sir Miles.

"Yes," she said, brightening. "A disguise. I like that." She smiled wanly.

"What would you say to a masked ball, then, Miss Lacy?" asked Eastham. He led the conversation back to the pleasures of the season, and Warne took care not to alarm Miss Lacy again. She made no obvious slips, but in a nature as open as hers there were still signs. She was hiding something,

something that had not come out in the story her
mother had so carelessly spread.

When the group around the girl broke up, he
turned to Mrs. Bowen. She stood but made no move
to speak to her aunt's guests as they took their
leave. Just such distance separated them that he
was sure she had heard every word of the conversation, but for him to cross to her, to take any
notice of the chaperone, sitting apart, would call
attention to her and raise doubts about his intentions. She was safe from his questions, and when
her gaze met his, he knew she knew it.

Susannah walked early. A cold, dense mist
shrouded the park. Her brown pelisse and a mul-
berry muffler were insufficient warmth for true
comfort, but the pleasure of being alone and moving freely was worth numb fingers and a reddened
nose. She stuck to a narrow footpath over the coarse
dry grass rather than the main tracks. She had no
wish to be ridden down by some gentleman out
for an early gallop, and she could not expect to be
noticed in the fog. The quiet, the chill, the loneli-
ness suited her purpose admirably, for she meant
to sort out her thoughts.

Juliet's indifference to eligible gentlemen made
Susannah uneasy. She had lain awake much of the
night imagining the end of the season, when she
would not be welcome to return to Uncle John and
no cottage would be waiting in Wincanton. She
would not apply to her brothers for help, and in any
case, Richard would never help her and Henry could
not. She would be forced to sell herself into some sort
of servitude unless she could bring Juliet around to
a sensible match. Still she would not despair.

She would compose a letter to Uncle John. He

would be impatient to hear how Juliet was getting on with the gentlemen he had chosen for her. Susannah would adopt a tone of cautious optimism. She would emphasize the amount of time Juliet had spent in Brentwood's company at that first ball and note that Lord Atwell had been prompt to call. She would even mention the unexceptional young men who had crowded Lady Lacy's drawing room the day before and indicate that she thought them worthy of investigation by Drummond and Drummond. It was too soon to point out that Brentwood and Atwell were unlikely to suit, and she would say absolutely nothing about the young highwayman or the Marquess of Warne.

He was not courting Juliet. Of that Susannah was sure, though her aunt was in a flutter at the prospect and he seemed to want the world to think so. Susannah knew the signs of a gentleman's interest in a lady and did not see them in Lord Warne's behavior toward Juliet. He was too rational, too shrewd. No, from Juliet he wanted information about the young man who had given out his card. Perhaps Susannah ought to volunteer what she knew, but she suspected society's impression of the marquess was accurate. He was ruthless and would offer an enemy no quarter. Their young rescuer had done nothing serious after all, and it had been Evelina who spread the story abroad. The highwayman could not be blamed for that. No, she would not tell Lord Warne anything. The episode was over, the young man had done them a kindness, and in time Juliet would forget him. Susannah would concentrate on finding Juliet a husband.

Warne swore at the thick, damp fog that slowed the pace of his morning run. His white running

clothes were soaked and clinging to him, and he
wanted the burn of a hard run. He needed to push
himself today. Yesterday the thief had handed one
of the cards to a clerk at Coutts's bank. The clerk
called his superior, but the man slipped away as
soon as the alarm was raised, and the clerk's recollections of the thief's appearance were vague. It
seemed that Warne's best chance of catching the
fellow was still Miss Lacy and his call upon her
had only frustrated him. The girl was hiding something. The mother seemed incapable of adding two
and two to make four, and he had twice missed his
chance to learn anything from the sober chaperone,
Mrs. Bowen.

At the Shalford ball he had been distracted by her
obvious desire to dance and had wasted his opportunity to question her, a lapse in concentration fatal
to success. And Mrs. Bowen knew it. He would not
make the same mistake again. At the very next
opportunity, he would question her directly about
the incident on the heath.

The wet black trunk of a tree emerged from the
mist in front of her, and Susannah halted and found
the path again where it swerved around the tree's
thick roots. She was picking her way over a gnarled
root when pounding footsteps startled her. She lifted
her head, trying to locate the sound in the mist. Then
a man all in white burst through the curtain of fog
at a run. Susannah stepped back, caught her heel
on a root, and staggered. The runner shortened his
stride and swerved, but Susannah stumbled directly into his path. They collided with a thump and
went down in a tangle of skirts and limbs.

She lay on her back in the thick damp grass and
looked up into Lord Warne's startled blue eyes.

"Mrs. Bowen . . . good morning," he said, his warm breath visible in the cold air. She could see the pulse in his throat and the fine dark stubble of beard along his jaw.

"Let me up."

"Of course," he answered, but he made no move to do so. He was looking at her as if he hadn't quite seen her before.

"You're not wearing your cap," he said.

She frowned and considered whether she might push him off of her. His sleeveless cambric shirt was mist-dampened and clung to his body, and the heat of that body, its weight pressed to hers, was melting her limbs. She raised her hands and shoved against his chest, but her arms had no strength.

When she let them fall, he pushed himself up with a quick pump of his powerful arms, but his hips and legs still held her pinned to the grass.

His eyes seemed to see her weakness, and she averted her gaze. "You must let me up, my lord," she said, striving for a command she did not feel.

He said nothing, and she studied his left arm, noting the course of a dark vein along the smooth curve of muscle as his breathing slowed.

When she dared to look at him again, the expression in his eyes had changed. "You were with Miss Lacy when the highwayman gave her my card," he said. He seemed to take no notice of the intimacy of their situation.

"Yes." Susannah tried to wriggle out from under him, but the weight of his hips against hers made a mockery of the attempt.

"What can you tell me about this man?"

"My lord!" she insisted. She balled her hands into fists and pressed against his chest. He did not budge.

"Age, manner, speech? Height, weight, mount? Features? Weapon? Left—or right-handed?"

"Let me up," she demanded.

"When you promise to answer my questions," he countered. He sank lower, resting now on his elbows, covering more of her body with his own. Her breath caught in her throat.

Warne knew he had to release her. It was foolish and not the part of a gentleman to take advantage as he was, but his mind seemed unable to command his limbs. His body, recognizing what his mind had sought to deny, urged the small movements that would bring him closer still. She grew quiet under him as if she understood what he was feeling. Her wide sweet mouth beckoned him.

"I'm going to kiss you."

"No," she said, but her pulse raced in answer to his words.

He took her chin and held it. She closed her eyes, willing herself not to tremble. His mouth touched hers, lightly. A stinging tear welled up and rolled hotly down her cold cheek. She had not been kissed in ten years.

Immediately her captor released her, pushing to his feet. She sat up and brushed away the tears. He held out a lean hand to help her up, but she shook her head. He stood there, his white garments clinging scandalously to his lithe form, and she averted her gaze, determined not to let him touch her again.

"That was unpardonable of me, Mrs. Bowen. Please allow me to help you up."

She shook her head again and folded her legs under her, rising to her knees, tugging at the tangle of her skirts. When she was on her feet, she bid him good day, but he stepped into her path.

"If you wish to see your charge *safely* wed, Mrs. Bowen, then you cannot want her to have any connection with the man I am asking about."

"It was likely some wager," she said. She stood, conscious of the marquess's scrutiny, and turned her attention to the state of her cloak and skirts.

"I doubt it." He looked at her as if weighing his next words. "My cards were stolen from the printer a fortnight ago."

Susannah looked at him directly. It was plain why people could think him hard and call him the Iron Lord. She was used to the blue of Juliet's eyes or even Aunt Evelina's, but blue eyes lighted by the marquess's intelligence and will were something else, cold as a March wind, she thought.

"Very well," she said.

"Let's walk then," he suggested.

She nodded, and he offered his arm, apparently forgetting that it was quite bare. When she only stared, he laughed, and the harsh blue disappeared at once.

"A stolen kiss and the impropriety of offering a lady an uncovered arm. Will you forgive me for that, too?" he asked.

Susannah lowered her gaze, determined not to blush at his easy reminder of their kiss. He bowed for her to precede him, and when she did, he followed.

"Your highwayman is young, well-spoken, gentlemanly in manner, acquainted with Shakespeare," she told him. "And I suspect, of a romantic disposition." She gave him a measuring stare. "We could see little of him in the dark, but he is of your height at least and deep-voiced. He must be accounted a fair shot, for he winged our other attacker neatly, and you may acquit him of cowardice."

"He said nothing of his purpose?"

"Nothing. He was dressed for the adventure and must have followed us from Staines. Perhaps he saw Juliet there. She was making a fuss."

"Has she seen him in London?"

"Of course not."

"You would recognize him?"

"The height, the voice, I think. He had a . . . touch of a Scot accent." They negotiated a rough place where the path crossed more roots, and Susannah thought of the way the rumors about their adventure had been distorted by gossip.

"Let me ask you a question, my lord."

"Ask."

"Could you have a son? An unacknowledged son?"

"No."

Susannah said nothing, only looked at him.

"Mrs. Bowen, I am not claiming unsullied virtue. You, at any rate, would not believe me. But the man you described to me must be near twenty. My sins are of more recent date. A little arithmetic clears me of being the father of your highwayman."

"Then why the note on the card?" she asked.

"It refers to my father, not my son," he said stiffly. "He and I were at war for nearly seventeen years."

So it was true, Susannah thought. He had bought his father's vowels, ruined his own father. She wondered what had caused such bitterness. "But your father is dead now, isn't he?" she asked.

"Yes, but the rule he lived by—*no score left unpaid*—seems to explain the cards. I think the highwayman meant to repay me for an injury I did my father. Eight or nine years ago, I held up my father's mistress on Hounslow Heath one evening."

"You think your father arranged some revenge beyond the grave?"

"He had friends, Mrs. Bowen, who were ruined with him. I am investigating them."

They had come to one of the main paths, and the fog was lifting a little. Susannah halted and turned to him. "I am sorry, Lord Warne, if my aunt's indiscretion contributed to your trouble with this thief. I have told you what I know, and I wish you luck in finding the man."

"Thank you, Mrs. Bowen."

"Good day," she said.

Warne watched her stride off. He had got what he wanted from Susannah Bowen, an account of Miss Lacy's meeting with the thief. Now he wanted more.

Hill's Boxing and Fencing Academy in Stanhope Street drew precisely the patrons Kirby was looking for—young gentlemen who wanted to improve their skills before attempting Jackson's, and fighters of promise who would leave Hill's to make their names at establishments like Cribb's Parlor. Unlike Jackson, Hill did not spar with his students. Rather he observed them carefully and set matches for them with each other, and for the Sunday match he picked the week's best. He was a small man with a pitted face, a loud harsh voice, and a genius for abusing his students until they could make of violence a dance of light feet and quick hands.

Among the young gentlemen Kirby introduced himself as an equal, claiming to be one of a numerous if obscure family from Yorkshire, educated at Edinburgh in the classics. It was sufficient disguise for such company as there were no scholars in the group and no one knew Warne by sight. It helped, too, that he could speak of Miss Lacy. He saw that he might gain entry into the ballrooms of London in the company of these new friends.

They dubbed him the Sinister Scot for his left, and he set to work to make the Sunday match so that Hill would bring him to Cribb's notice. Tom Cribb would remember Warne. With Cribb he would leave his father's card.

10

When Susannah next saw Lord Warne, he was in a party of a dozen or more ladies and gentlemen moving about the dim shed that housed Lord Elgin's marbles. Evelina pointed out the exceptionally pretty girl in Warne's party as the heiress Miss Nevins.

"Surely, Warne isn't thinking of her," Evelina whispered to Juliet. "If she's the least like her mama, he'll be sorry. There's Esther, dears, I must talk to her."

"Let's just wander, Susannah," Juliet suggested. She looked about with apparent interest. It had been Juliet's idea to visit the exhibit, and Susannah, though surprised by her cousin's desire to see the statues, had been more than willing to go. She watched Juliet stroll off and saw her greet an old gentleman, leaning on a cane. Really, her charge was behaving better than she had expected.

Susannah took her bearings and crossed to one end of the frieze. She was marvelling at the ancient world carved in stone, the figures so lifelike it seemed they might spring from the marble, when she became conscious of a gentleman at her side. She turned to find Lord Warne.

"Do you think Parliament should pay Elgin the asking price for his treasures?" he asked, looking not at her but at the frieze.

"They are priceless."

"They give you pleasure?"

"Oh yes." She glanced up. He was watching her with a steady regard, and she lowered her gaze again.

"As your morning walk gives you pleasure?"

Susannah nodded, keeping her eyes fixed on the arm of a reclining figure, surely one of the gods. Had Warne seen her this morning? She had not noticed him in the park though she had been conscious every time she walked that he might be there. Always the park reminded her of him, and now the naked male arm in front of her with its swell of muscle and stretch of sinew recalled Warne's arms as she had seen them that morning.

"Lord Warne," she said briskly, shaking off her foolish awareness of him. "Why are you talking to me? I told you what I knew of your card thief."

"But, Mrs. Bowen," he said, taking her arm and drawing her along to stand before the figure of a tall, headless goddess. "Should we not acknowledge one another? After all we have a common aim this season and must compare our progress."

Susannah gave him a frankly incredulous look. "What aim could we possibly share?"

"Each of us is choosing a spouse," he said.

"I'm not looking for a husband," she protested.

He seemed to be enjoying her astonishment. "You are choosing for your cousin, I for myself," he explained. "Of course, that means I am likely to be more successful than you, since I need only please myself, while you are endeavoring to please another."

"We are neither of us buying hats, my lord," Susannah said with some asperity.

Warne laughed, and Susannah could not help but

admire the pleasant way laughter altered his face. "That's a good thing." He traced the rim of her gray silk bonnet with one finger. "Your selection of suitors for Miss Lacy so far speaks of extreme caution, Mrs. Bowen."

"And yours, Lord Warne, speaks of remarkable modesty. Do you think only the most mercenary or the most insensible will have you? I thought you had a better opinion of yourself."

His face took on a wry expression. "I have it on good authority that my reputation limits my choices. What do you think I should be looking for in a wife?"

"My lord, I would not presume to advise you."

"But you've been married, Mrs. Bowen. Surely, you have some opinion of the qualities that promote marital felicity?"

Susannah looked at him. It was another of his traps. "You want me to say love, my lord, and then you will ask me what—"

"—what *could* Brentwood possibly have to do with love?" he finished.

Susannah composed herself. "Love is dangerous. There are other grounds for marriage."

"Such as?"

"Such as respect and amiability and . . ."

"Desire," he offered.

Susannah made the mistake then of looking up into his eyes. The heat in them reminded her of the moment in the park when he had bent his head to hers. He too, was clearly thinking of that moment. His gaze dropped to her lips.

"Warne," a female voice called. He glanced over Susannah's shoulder.

"Excuse me, Mrs. Bowen," he said. "I hope you enjoy the exhibit." He strolled off as if they had exchanged the merest commonplaces, while Susannah stood quite still trying to calm a quivering in her nerves.

Warne stared out the window of his breakfast room. Mrs. Bowen had avoided him this morning. There was no mistaking that slim brown shape or the concealing hood. And there had been that slight pause in her stride, a check and a change of path. He should not mind it, yet he did. He had no doubt that she was the cause of the current irksomeness of his self-imposed celibacy. He was unable to rid himself of recollections of that startling moment in the park when he'd found himself lying on her in a parody of his true desires.

Even away from her his mind seemed to have lost its quickness and staying power. Bellaby's absence did not help. Neil always credited Warne with the intuitions that had made them rich, but Warne wondered if his friend's ideas weren't more necessary to his thinking than he had realized. Without Neil it was proving difficult to solve the puzzle of the card thief.

In a fortnight he had achieved little. True he had cut the man off from the banks, and even the pawn shops, but after the episode at Coutts's, the fellow had not been seen anywhere. He, meanwhile, was no more successful in his search for a bride. Girls making their come-out were, as Bellaby had predicted, too shy for his taste. Those who had been on the town more than a season, or widows like Ann Trentfield, seemed too calculating. He was made aware that his title, wealth, and ability to sire an heir were the qualities women were weighing against the rumors of his ruthlessness. Still others seemed to wonder if he would be interested in a different sort of arrangement. Meanwhile, Susannah Bowen surrounded her cousin with Brentwood, Atwell, and their ilk.

Warne turned from the window and poured a cup of coffee. He had had a letter from Bellaby, detailing what Neil had discovered in Berkshire from the servants who accompanied Miss Lacy and Mrs. Bowen to London. It told essentially the same story Mrs. Bowen had finally revealed. A young man with a touch of the Scot about him had stopped the Lacy coach. He saved the ladies from two low thieves and requested a kiss from Juliet Lacy, but had yielded to Mrs. Bowen's protests and merely left the young lady with one of the stolen cards.

The young man, whoever he was, had set out to hold up a coach. His clothes, the time and place, and his weapon proclaimed his intention. That much Warne believed the fellow had been hired to do, but he suspected that the would-be highwayman had departed from instructions, distracted by the loveliness of Miss Lacy. No more cards had appeared in a fortnight, and Warne could only conclude that whoever was behind this scheme of revenge was dissatisfied with the highwayman's performance. Warne's own investigation had revealed that Jopp was not behind the appearance of any of the stolen cards. Jopp had suffered an apoplectic fit of some sort and retired to his sister's farm. That still left his father's man of business, solicitor, and bailiff, all men who had remained loyal to the old marquess and suffered with him as Warne succeeded. And perhaps some lord who had been ruined with the old marquess.

A knock on the breakfast-room door interrupted

his thoughts at this point, and when he answered, Madsen, his secretary, entered.

The young man was one of Rumsford's nephews, with a good head for numbers, and like Bellaby, an eye for detail. His fair head was bent, and he was frowning at a letter he held in his left hand, his blue eyes shifting back and forth as they did when he was thinking hard.

"Sir, you've had the oddest letter come, from a Mr. Meyer."

"The tailor?" Warne asked.

Madsen nodded. "He respectfully requests that he not be made a party to the sort of economic warfare in which your lordship and your late father indulged. He asks that your son's custom not be a cause for reprisals against established tradesmen honestly plying their trades." Madsen looked up as if he had something very important to communicate.

"Go on."

"It made no sense to me, sir, but as I looked at this month's duns, I found six from tradesmen you've never patronized. That is, I've never seen their bills before."

"Six?" asked Warne, reaching for the sheets his secretary was holding.

"Not just Meyer, but Davidson, Poole, Pike for trousers, Townley . . ." He handed over the sheaf of papers. "There are bills for a coat, two pair of pantaloons, a full suit of evening wear, boots, a hat, gloves, and other furnishings—all from establishments you've never traded with, sir."

Warne examined the papers. All were dated since the theft of his cards. He stood up. "Madsen, call on these tradesmen and find out what you can about the person who made these purchases. Each will likely produce one of my cards. Settle any accounts, and if they are willing, collect the cards and bring them to me."

Madsen looked surprised. "Settle, sir? You never . . . That is I should not like to put out money for goods you never received."

Warne smiled. "A sound principle, Madsen. Nevertheless, do this for me."

"Of course, sir," the young man replied. He gave a nod, accepted the papers, and withdrew.

So it was not over after all, Warne thought. The round of cards to tailors furthered his suspicion that his father had planned this revenge. Who else knew the steps their war with one another had taken? But the thief or his accomplice had made one mistake. When Madsen returned, he would be able to tell Warne exactly what the fellow looked like—down to the size of his boots. And that information Warne would take to Miss Lacy and Mrs. Bowen. Which ball would they be attending tonight? He thought of the stack of invitations on his desk. It should be an easy matter to determine Evelina Lacy's preference for the evening.

Kirby fumbled with the lock. His fingers were stiff, every muscle ached, the cut over his left eye stung, and he was hungry again. From across the landing came a savory smell, to which his treacherous belly responded. Mrs. Hayter had fed him more than once in the past fortnight, but he couldn't accept another meal from her even if there was no food in his rooms. He hadn't had time this week for any of the odd jobs that filled his purse, and he had spent the last of his blunt in a display of careless generosity, buying drinks for his friends from Hill's. That had been a piece of foolishness which had obliged him to listen to Alan Garrett describe the pleasure of dancing with Juliet Lacy. It was plain she was having a fine season and had forgotten her highwayman. Kirby had not had time to seek her out as he'd planned, and she had not returned to Lackington's though he had gone as often as he could.

He reminded himself that revenge was his purpose. He had purchased a gentleman's wardrobe with his father's cards and had earned a spot in Hill's Sunday match. If he had had a setback at Coutts's bank, if he seemed alone in the world, if he was sure Miss Lacy had forgotten him, those were tests of his resolve. He dropped the key and swore under his breath. Behind him Mrs. Hayter's door opened.

"Kirby," she called softly.

He turned to face her. "Evening, ma'am."

"Ma'am?" she said. "Oh dear, we're back to that."

"Not at all . . . Molly," he assured her, but he felt his face heat. He had not embarrassed himself in her presence again, but those breasts disturbed his dreams. If he fell asleep imagining Juliet Lacy, he would wake roused and dreaming of Mrs. Hayter's creamy flesh. Tonight she was dressed for an evening engagement in a diaphanous gown of white, a deep green silk shawl about her shoulders. Her hair was up, like the ringleted ladies of Attica, he thought. Except that those beauties of long ago would have bared and rouged their breasts, his mother had explained. He looked away.

"You've been at Hill's?"

Kirby should have guessed that she'd know. She seemed to know everything about the people in the lodging house. He nodded.

"Then," she said, "you must need a glass of wine and a bath."

"A bath?" He retrieved his key, covering his surprise at the offer.

"Of course, and something for that cut above your eye. Come on."

"But you are going out, aren't you?"

"Only to Draycot's," she said with a shrug. "And I need not hurry."

The din of one of Draycot's parties was already discernible, coming up from below.

It was easy to give in. From the open door behind her came light and warmth and the smell of stew, and there could be no harm in *looking* at Mrs. Hayter. She was dressed and the shawl covered her breasts. He followed her.

One of her hovering maids brought wine, and the second brought a tray with a steaming bowl and slices of bread. He was encouraged to eat and tell the tale of his fight.

"Not thinking of a career in the ring, are you?" she asked.

"Nae," he answered, but offered no more.

"Yet you made Hill's Sunday match," she said. "You must not be modest but tell me all about it." She pressed the wine glass into his hand.

As before he found it easy to talk, and when she reminded him of the bath, he heard himself agree. The wine made him feel light-headed and lazy. She led him from her drawing room down a hall toward the back of the suite and pushed open a door, and the scene that met his gaze brought to mind lines from Odysseus's great adventure—"A maid came with richly colored rugs to throw on seat and chairback. A second . . . mixed wine as tawny-mild as honey . . . another came bearing

water, and lit a blaze under a cauldron. By and by
it bubbled, and when the dazzling brazen vessel
seethed she filled a bathtub to my waist . . ." He
could not remember where in the hero's adventures
Odysseus had met such luxury, but surely its equal
was before him in Mrs. Hayter's bedroom.

The floor was carpeted with the rich, dark pat-
terns of Turkey or Persia. A fire burned brightly in
the hearth, a copper tub gleamed in its light, steam
rising from the shimmering water. She led him to a
bench with a folded towel, and the maids pulled a
standing screen to one side of the gleaming tub.

"Take as long as you like," she advised him, and
withdrew.

He stared at the richness of her private apartment. She had hinted at some tragedy that had
brought her down in the world, but behind the
shabby exterior of the building she lived in comfort
that surpassed any Kirby had seen outside of the
great houses. Steam curled lazily from the bath. He
sat and removed his boots, then stripped and eased
into the tub. The heat was just bearable and went
directly to his aches. He rested his head against the
copper lip. His mind spun dizzily, and he closed his
eyes.

When he opened them, the bath had cooled and
Mrs. Hayter was sitting on the bench. He sat up
with an abruptness that sent the water lapping at
the sides of the tub.

"It's not wise to fall asleep in the bath," she
remarked.

Kirby could not look away. Her shawl was gone,
and the firelight revealed the fullness of her shape
through the white gown. Sometime in his doze his
thoughts had turned from his revenge to Miss Lacy.
Now her lovely image faded, and the gentle rocking

of the water against his naked flesh awoke desires he had been unwilling to admit.

"I've warmed a towel for you," said Mrs. Hayter. She smiled and left him.

He stepped from the tub and grabbed the towel, applying it in long hurried strokes, looking for his clothes, but they had disappeared. He wrapped the towel about his waist, thinking furiously. Did she want him to stay? He glanced at the bed not more than a few feet away.

"A robe?" offered his hostess, reappearing from behind the screen.

Like a waiting manservant she held up a black silk wrapper, but what he saw was the smooth white curve of her arms. He thought of questions he had not asked of his mother, of jokes he had pretended to understand, of Ares and Aphrodite, the adulterers, under Hephaestus's golden chain and all the gods come to see. He thought of all that had been denied him by his father's absence in his childhood. Anger and lust united.

He turned his back, released the towel at his waist and slipped his arms into the robe. When he had tied it, he faced her.

"You want to kiss me don't you," she said. In her eyes was the patient, sympathetic look with which she had listened to his story.

He nodded. He grasped her shoulders, pulling her towards him. Fleetingly he thought of Juliet Lacy, but the wine fogged his mind and Mrs. Hayter's mouth opened under his. He slid his hands downward, filling them with soft ripe flesh. His breath came hot and harsh, and he pulled back, to see what he touched. Mrs. Hayter guided his hand to the slender ribbon at the gathers of her bodice, and he loosed it, brushing aside the thin cloth. He stared at the white flesh, the dusky rose peaks.

She took him by the hand and pulled him gently toward the bed. Then he remembered where Odysseus was when he took that bath. The hero's words came back, "It is I you hold, enticing into your chamber, to your dangerous bed, to take my manhood when you have me stripped . . ." Circe's hall.

Kirby sought to hold onto the thought of danger, but Mrs. Hayter touched her mouth to his, beguiling him and driving him to press his body to hers.

Dimly he heard pounding and the whisper of slippered feet scurrying. "Molly! Sweet Molly! Open your door. Open your—" The loud pounding obscured the words. There were several voices, one of them Draycot's. The actor was drunk, to judge from the sound. The woman in Kirby's arms stiffened and drew back from him. He opened his eyes, surprised to see Molly Hayter.

"Wait for me," she urged him, her fingers cleverly putting her bodice back in order. The shouting and pounding continued, and Mrs. Hayter hurried away. He heard her voice in the hall and the voices of the little maids.

The black robe had fallen open, and he stood exposed in his lust. Juliet Lacy's image came back to him then, sweet and guileless, and he groaned. He didn't want Molly Hayter. The muddle of anger, lust, and wine cleared, and he took a deep shaky breath. He raised his arm and rubbed the sleeve of the silk robe across his lips, cleansing them of the taste of Mrs. Hayter. He had to see Miss Lacy, to kiss *her*. He stepped from behind the screen, began looking for his clothes, and found them on a chair in the dark.

11

Susannah emerged from the cloakroom of the Royston mansion with serious misgivings about the evening ahead. Even in her season, Lord and Lady Royston's ball had been a notorious event. Once a year the earl and his lady opened their garden and the many rooms of their large mansion to the whole of the *ton*, and expected approximately the behavior suited to Vauxhall. Only the high sticklers stayed away. Ten years before, Susannah had been thoroughly kissed in the gardens below the terrace; it had been one small step in her seduction.

She could not tell Evelina that, of course, and her objections to the ball had not swayed her aunt or her cousin. They had received vouchers for Almack's, and Evelina was convinced that Juliet would have a great triumph there, but Susannah could not help thinking that it was too soon to be sure of Juliet's success and too careless of her reputation to bring her to the Roystons'.

Juliet, herself, seemed consumed by an impatient longing for some decisive moment that would fix her fate. In little more than a fortnight the girl had become adept at judging the character of a gathering. Tonight she had chosen a sophisticated overdress of pale blue bordered with a deep lapis cord over a muslin slip. At Susannah's side she adjusted her long gloves and eyed the other guests with open curiosity.

"Look," she said, leaning toward Susannah, "it's Mrs. Elvers, Royston's mistress. She's not as pretty as I thought she'd be."

"Juliet," protested Susannah, "where did you hear that piece of scandal?"

"It's common knowledge, Susannah," said Evelina. "I wonder that Louisa Elvers does not simply move in. The place is so large, Lady R. would be less likely to meet her rival here than in town."

"Is Lady Royston so complacent about her husband's infidelities?" Susannah asked.

"Don't be prudish, dear. With Sir Roger Hume to console her Lady R. can be quite complacent. No doubt he's here as well."

"Then perhaps Byron and his Augusta should come; even they might find a welcome," Susannah could not resist adding.

Her aunt stared at her, but made no reply, and they moved with the crowd into the Royston ballroom. The high-ceilinged room stretched along one wing of the building and opened across the rear of the mansion to a row of connecting salons, which had been turned into something of a Parisian street scene with vendors' carts, lampposts, flower stands, potted trees, and tables under awnings. Between sets guests might stroll along this artificial avenue or step out onto the terrace and down into the garden below, where the paths were marked by strings of paper lanterns.

Evelina hardly noticed, pointing out instead the more notorious of the Roystons' guests. Abruptly she broke off, saying, "There's Ann Trentfield. I must catch her. She is sure to know all about the royal wedding plans. Juliet, dear, stay with Susannah."

Susannah watched her aunt scurry off and then looked about her. Apparently there were no seats for chaperones. Nor did Susannah see a place where she and Juliet could settle and wait for gentlemen to request a dance. They began a circuit of the ballroom, feeling more and more buffeted by the laughter, the scents, and the bustle of the other guests until Susannah was relieved to see Lord Brentwood approaching.

But Juliet said, "Not here, too. Can't I be free of Papa's choices for one evening?"

Susannah regarded his lordship's earnest face and recalled the marquess saying *"Brentwood."* In her season she would not have tolerated the prosy peer for an hour. "Let's find you another partner then, Juliet. Someone with a less wooden wit."

Juliet blinked, as if she couldn't believe what Susannah suggested. Then she smiled. Susannah indicated an opening in the crowd, and she and Juliet slipped away.

On the far side of the ballroom they encountered Alan Garrett. He sought to present some friends of his, but had apparently lost them in the confusion of so many guests. To Susannah he looked a trifle on the go, but he was certainly an unexceptional partner for Juliet and he engaged her at once for the next set.

Kirby entered the Royston mansion with Garrett, Newbury, and a half dozen other friends from Hill's, whom he'd met as they finished dinner. The wine they'd consumed had made them ready to accept the sketchy account he offered to explain why he hadn't joined them earlier. Then they were off to the ball, never doubting that he had been invited. He fell in with their plans. If nothing else they would get him to the West End, and if the party proved to lack Miss Lacy, he would search for her elsewhere.

But Garrett discovered her shortly after their arrival. It had required some quick footwork on Kirby's part to fade into the crowd as his friend approached the girl. It would not do to be presented to Miss Lacy with others there to witness the encounter. He was meeting her for the first time with no disguise and could not be sure she would not give the game away. He thought it wiser to bide his time and get her alone, and the Royston party seemed contrived to help him achieve his object. The din, the milling guests, the number of rooms, the dozen doors opening on a wide terrace, and the paths below in the darkened garden fairly encouraged dalliance. He moved around the ballroom, observing her dance with Garrett and planning his strategy.

Susannah could not be sure precisely when she lost Juliet. Her cousin had danced a lively country dance with Mr. Garrett and then accepted that gentleman's arm. A turn about the ballroom would bring them back to Susannah, but she had been distracted momentarily by the start of a waltz. When she looked for Juliet again, the girl had vanished. And the press of people made a search difficult.

Everywhere Susannah turned she saw toques and turbans and waving plumes, not the maidenly curls Juliet wore. To progress through the crowd it was necessary to say "pardon me," in a voice much louder than her accustomed speaking voice, and even then, her fellow guests were not inclined to make way for her. She doubted there was another lace cap in the place. Nevertheless, she had reached the first of the salons along the rear of the house when she encountered Lord Warne.

"Mrs. Bowen," he said, blocking her way, taller than those around them, and dressed in black pantaloons and a black evening coat. "Looking for a partner?"

"Of course not."

"Pity."

The regret in his tone stopped her, and her gaze settled on his mouth. Her treacherous memory betrayed her instantly with a recollection of his kiss in the park. His contained elegance now was nothing like the loose cambric shirt he had worn in the park, but Susannah was no less aware of the man under the clothes. Her pulse unaccountably raced.

"You've lost your cousin, I think," he said. His gaze seemed to note her distress.

She touched her cap, making sure the circle of lace was properly settled on her head. "We have merely been parted by the movement of the crowd."

"Your eyes betray your alarm, Mrs. Bowen. Shall I help you look for Miss Lacy?"

"Have you seen her?"

He shook his head.

"Excuse me, then, my lord." She stepped to one side, intent on passing him, but with a slight move he again blocked her way. Not touching her, but so close, she was suddenly consious of the rough edge of her lace tuck against her sensitive breasts and the thin silk of her gown clinging to her hips and thighs. A wanton and mortifying heat flashed through her, and she raised her chin to give him a level stare, but the marquess's blue eyes did not waver.

"I can help, you know, and your efforts will look less obvious if you are seen strolling on my arm rather than struggling through the press on your own. You have no wish to create a scandal, I take it."

"None," she said tightly.

He turned and offered his arm, and she took it. Then with a word to the gentleman in front of them, he began to clear a path for them.

As they passed into the first of the large salons along the rear of the house, he asked about Juliet's dress and the persons of her acquaintance who were or who might be supposed to be at the Royston ball. They saw Evelina in conversation with their host. But no sign of Juliet.

In the second of the large rooms they found Garrett in a crowd of gentlemen hovering about a stunning young woman. He had the same besotted look he wore when talking to Juliet. Susannah clutched Warne's arm, and he drew her closer. Why had she let Juliet dance with Garrett? If Brentwood had danced with Juliet, he would never have left her side. She would be safe.

"That's Letitia Duren," Warne whispered in her ear, "an actress. Was Miss Lacy with Garrett earlier?"

Susannah nodded.

"What is to become of your charge's *safe* marriage?" he asked.

"Do not joke, sir," said Susannah. "My cousin will pay for imprudent behavior the rest of her life."

"As you have done?"

It was so sudden and unexpected a hit that Susannah had raised her gaze to his before she realized how such an action must give her away. She

halted and would have pulled away, but he covered
her hand with his own. Under his, hers trembled.

"I am living as I choose to live. A woman, my
lord, is more vulnerable to attacks on her good
name than any man and must live more circum-
spectly."

"Byron would argue with you."

"But Caro Lamb would not."

"Brentwood is not the answer for your cousin,"
he argued.

"And you can tell me who is?"

"Should Miss Lacy take a leaf from your book
and wear caps and never dance?"

"Choices appropriate to my age and station, my
lord."

"But not to your spirit. I have seen your eyes when
a waltz is danced and your unfettered stride in the
park, Mrs. Bowen. Your spirit is tightly reined in."

"That is my choice, Lord Warne," she replied.

Kirby took out one of his father's cards inscribed
with his message of revenge. It was the work of a
few minutes to command a footman to take it to
Miss Lacy. As he hoped it would, the card roused
her attention. She was standing with Garrett and
the others, and he saw her glance about with apparently no more than idle curiosity, but he held his
breath when he felt the approach of her gaze. At
any moment she would see him standing in a doorway to the terrace. Just then, their eyes met, and he
felt the jolt of recognition that hit her. He backed
out into the night and waited.

An interminable interval passed, in which he
could hear nothing except his own heartbeat, and
then she stepped through the doors. He caught her
hand and pulled her toward him.

"'If I profane with my unworthiest hand,'" he said.

"Is that Romeo again?" she asked, looking at him with open curiosity.

He swallowed. "Yes. Will you walk with me in the garden?"

"How did you get in here?"

"'With love's light wings did I o'erperch these walls.'"

"But it's not safe, is it? Your . . . father told me they hang highwaymen," she said gravely.

He stiffened. "I want to kiss you," he said.

"I know," she answered, accepting his lead and turning with him toward the terrace steps.

At the foot of the stairs they found a grassy path and followed it by the light of the paper lanterns until Kirby found a place where a break in the shrubbery allowed them to slip through. They stepped into a sort of alcove between the bushes and the high wall of the Royston garden. Without hesitation he took her in his arms and pressed his mouth firmly to hers. She tasted sweet like apples or berries, and she kissed him with an honest relish he could not mistake. He forgot the taste of wine and anger and lust, and he knew he would have to see her again. When they paused to draw breath, she framed his face with her hands. There was no lantern near, but in the light from the great rooms above them there was no hiding who he was.

"You look just like him, you know," she said solemnly.

"No, I don't," he answered harshly, turning his head. He meant to pull back, but found his lips against her palm and pressed a kiss there. Her hand coaxed him to turn and look at her again.

"Does he know you are here?" she whispered.

"No, and he must not find out."

She said nothing, but he read the questions in her eyes.

"I will tell you what I can when I can," he said. "Meet me tomorrow?"

She nodded. "And I won't say a word. But wouldn't you be safer in disguise?" she asked.

"Probably," he admitted. "Tonight I . . . wanted you to see me."

She smiled, and he drew her close again.

Warne looked over the heads of the other guests and halted. He and Mrs. Bowen had come to the threshold of the last of the rooms across the rear of the mansion. Juliet Lacy appeared at the terrace doors, partially concealed by a potted lime tree. Warne slipped behind a large gentleman, pulling Mrs. Bowen after him. They could not be seen, but he could still see Miss Lacy.

"There's your cousin now," he said.

Mrs. Bowen stood on tiptoe and looked over his shoulder. "She's been in the garden," she said in a stricken voice that made him turn to her. Her dark eyes were wild with alarm, and she attempted to push past him, but he held her back.

"However desperate you are to prevent harm to your cousin's reputation, dashing to her side in this crowd would not be wise," he said.

She lowered her gaze in acquiescence, and the familiar gesture distracted him momentarily. Her fears went beyond a conscientious chaperone's concern for an impulsive girl. If they were alone, if he had time, he knew he could discover the secret that fettered Susannah Bowen's proud spirit.

Instead, he merely said, "Your cousin looks safe and sound."

Miss Lacy straightened her gloves and her skirts and touched the curls that framed her face. She glanced around again, and seemed satisfied with her appearance. Then she tilted her head to one side as if listening intently. She gave a small nod, apparently assenting to something someone behind her in the darkness said, put a deliberate smile on her face and entered the salon.

Warne stiffened. Perhaps Susannah Bowen had good reason for her distress. Whoever had spoken to Miss Lacy from the darkness beyond the bright salon, it was not one of her usual suitors, but someone she felt obliged to conceal and protect with her careful return to the party, someone who could not accompany her into the lighted rooms of the Royston mansion. He must see who that someone was.

Fifty people or more occupied the space between him and that doorway, and he was calculating how he might pass through them unobtrusively when a voice spoke at his side.

"Looking for your little charge, Mrs. Bowen?" Ann Trentfield asked, her sharp eyes clearly noting their clasped hands.

Warne stepped from behind the portly gentleman, drawing Susannah with him. "Actually," he said, "Miss Lacy is just there, Mrs. Trentfield, waiting for us to join her for refreshments. Will you excuse us, ma'am?"

Kirby watched his father greet Miss Lacy and felt a raging, intolerable desire to rush into the room, to brandish a sword and wave it in his father's face, to pull Miss Lacy back into the darkness where she had belonged, however briefly, to him. And he felt shocked into immobility. He was as near his father as he had ever been, and he could not deny his resemblance to the man. The slanting brows, the blade of a nose, the eyes. They were of a height and there was no mistaking the shape of his head, even the movements. How could he so resemble a man he hated? How could he hate a man whose face he bore?

But the man could not court Juliet Lacy. She was too good, too innocent, too trusting to be wed to Warne.

Reason returned. He must not reveal himself here, but somehow he would let his father know they had been there together in the same ballroom. He could send a footman with a card as he had done to catch Miss Lacy's notice, but that would not cause his father any embarrassment. Besides he wanted to be sure of his escape before he alerted his father to his presence.

He made his way to Garrett and the others, conscious now of the probability that his looks could betray him. His friends assured him they meant to stay to the end, and Letitia Duren, who had seen him once or twice at the theatre, looked at him as if recognition just eluded her grasp. Kirby told them he'd met some cousins and was going on to another party.

Then he hurried down the great stair to the room set aside for gentlemen's hats and cloaks. Three footmen were chatting idly, but seeing him there, one jumped up. The fellow's quick subservience gave Kirby an idea.

"Warne," he said.

The man scurried off to search among the rows of hats. Kirby stepped further into the room. He had perhaps a dozen of the stolen cards on him and drew them out of his pocket. He began to pace as if impatient. A score of hats were within his reach. He dropped a card in a hat here, a hat there. When the footman brought his father's hat, he took it and settled it on his head, a perfect fit. He gave the fellow a coin, and one of the cards, and strode off whistling.

12

Sometime between their return from the ball at two and Susannah's rising at six, it rained. A brief, furious storm left the park strewn with twigs and blossoms, the blades of grass fresh and shiny. Susannah took an unfamiliar path and kept her hood up. She doubted she would encounter Lord Warne this particular morning, but she had no wish to be confronted by him.

For a moment he had been almost kind, but his kindness was as dangerous as his wrath. He had come too close to understanding her. Then when they had found Juliet and seen her reply to someone in the darkness, Warne had assumed again the harsh aspect of the Iron Lord. It had been apparent that his real aim was to find the card thief and that somehow he blamed Susannah for the man's escape. He had watched Juliet with disquieting intensity and then abruptly left them.

Once home, however, Juliet refused to talk to Susannah about her disappearance. Susannah reminded her cousin of the strict code that ruled a lady's conduct in society and of her father's hopes for her. Juliet listened but remained unmoved. She claimed she did not need suitors and was not worried about mere reputation. That was well enough Susannah pointed out, for Juliet had very nearly thrown reputation away by stepping into the garden at such a ball. Lord Warne had been aware of Juliet's lapse and so had Ann Trentfield. If Mrs. Trentfield chose to be nasty about it, the *on dit* would be that Juliet was fast. Juliet repeated that she did not care. From that point on, Susannah had scolded and argued in vain. She could not decide which was more disturbing—Lord Warne's distrust or the nagging thought that the safe little cottage would never be hers.

But this morning with the world new and fresh, she understood Juliet's dissatisfaction. Brentwood and Garrett were not the sort of men that would do for her cousin. Her uncle had not chosen wisely at all, and Aunt Evelina's picks were no better. Her aunt admired a man with a sartorial dash but little substance. As unbookish as Juliet was, the girl still respected intelligence and must have it in the man she would marry. Juliet would need someone like Lord Warne, and Susannah was suddenly conscious that she had not written about him to her uncle as perhaps she should have.

Warne followed Susannah Bowen into the park, staying well back, and waiting until she had committed herself to a path before he drew near. He was sure she had left the ball late, but he never doubted she would walk. She had been to the park every day since the time they had collided in the fog. He had not approached her since that morning, but last night she had betrayed him, and this morning he wanted satisfaction.

When he recalled their desperate search for Miss Lacy, he realized Mrs. Bowen must have known her charge was meeting the thief. And she had effectively distracted him so that he had missed his chance to slip out to the terrace. He had then watched Miss Lacy surrounded by her usual court of young men, all known to him, and when he perceived the futility of his watch, he left.

In the cloakroom, he had encountered Maitland, who drew a laugh from everyone present by pulling one of the stolen cards from a gentleman's hat and asking, "My dear Warne, don't you know your own hat?"

When he asked for his hat and coat, however, the footman claimed to have given them to him already and produced another of the stolen cards. When questioned, the footman admitted the fellow might not have been Warne, but he was sure the gentleman had asked for Warne's things and he was like enough your lordship, like enough. Warne told Royston's servants that there would likely be an unclaimed coat and hat at the end of the evening and asked that those be delivered to his direction.

No score left unpaid. It came back to that. Well he had been made to feel foolish as he had no doubt made his father feel, but he would not be the maddened bull his father would have been. Once home he did not go to bed, but built up the fire in his library and considered what he knew about the card thief. The Royston footmen confirmed what Madsen had learned from the tailors. The fellow apparently resembled him and knew it because he had disguises at his disposal. Half the tradesmen had sworn they were dealing with a dark-haired man, while the others described a fair one. One tailor had detected a Scot phrase, and that tied the man to the highwayman who had accosted Miss Lacy. The only advantage Warne seemed to possess in this strange game was that his enemy, whoever he was, was smitten with Miss Lacy, and could not stay away. Miss Lacy would be the flame to draw the moth.

When the path took Susannah Bowen down into a secluded hollow north of the Serpentine, he circled around, moving swiftly so that he might meet her on the other side. She approached, apparently lost in thought, her hooded head bent.

"Good morning, Mrs. Bowen," he said.

She stopped abruptly and raised startled eyes to his. "Good day, Lord Warne," she replied, turning on her heel, clearly intending to retrace her steps.

He reached out and caught a fold of her cloak, checking her. She turned.

"I do not wish to talk to you, Lord Warne," she said. She looked pointedly at his hand clutching her cloak.

"But you will," he answered, releasing the garment. "For Miss Lacy's sake."

"Very well," she said primly, the wide mouth closed in a firm line.

"She has been seeing that highwayman," he said flatly.

"She has not." Her eyes flashed. "I know my duty. Miss Lacy does not go about unaccompanied."

"As you do?"

Her chin rose a fraction. "I am . . . a widow and may be permitted more license. My cousin has been in my company at all times."

"Except last night."

"You cannot think that she met your highwayman at the Roystons' ball. As rackety as they are, they would not have sent an invitation to a thief."

"No, but a bold thief, dressed as a gentleman, would find it little challenge to gain entré in that crowd. She not only met him. She's protecting him."

"Nonsense. That would be folly. Whoever she stepped outside with, it could not have been your man. You did not see him. How can you be sure he was even there?"

He reached in his pocket and pulled out the card that had been waiting for him in the cloakroom. He handed it to Mrs. Bowen. "Because he left his card."

She took the little card. Their fingers touched briefly, and even the light contact recalled the moment his body had been pressed to hers in the damp grass.

She stared at the card, and the defiant spirit seemed to drain out of her. "It seems you are right, Lord Warne. I will take care that Miss Lacy does not encounter your thief again." She nodded as if dismissing him and turned away.

"But she *must*," he said.

She stopped and looked over her shoulder at him. "I beg your pardon?"

"She must see him again, and you must arrange matters so that I may be there."

"My lord, are you proposing to use my cousin as a lure?" She had turned on him now, and her eyes had a martial light in them.

"I am," he said, as much for the satisfaction of rousing her as for the truth of it.

"You will not. It is unthinkable that she should be exposed to gossip for your purposes."

"Last night, Mrs. Bowen, your cousin exposed herself to gossip all on her own. Let her do it again."

"No."

They were glaring at one another now, and he

could not help admiring the flash in those dark eyes. He had jarred her out of her habit of lowering them, hiding the fire in them from notice, as the plain brown hood of her cloak covered her hair, hiding it from the light that would reveal its fiery strands.

"You are worried about her chances of making a *safe* marriage." He could not help the irony in his tone.

"Yes," she said fervently.

"And why," he said, closing the gap between them, "do you care so much for that? Her mama does not care. She does not care."

"Someone must," she said, but her voice lacked conviction and she looked away.

"Why you?" He paused. "Why do you care, Susannah?"

A tremor passed through her. "It is my duty."

He wanted to touch her, but he kept his voice harsh. "Then you will fail," he said. "Your cousin loves danger not prudence."

She looked up, "Oh you *are* cold. You deserve the title they give you. Iron Lord." She whirled and would have stepped away, but he caught her by the hand and spun her back and because she resisted, he drew her closer, pulling the slim, taut body up against his, holding her fast with an arm about her waist.

"Shall I tell you about iron, Mrs. Bowen, about how it is made? About the ore pried out of the earth with picks and drills and blasts? About the crushing and grinding of it? About the wedding of metal, and coke, black as hell, in a furnace as hot? You think me hard. I have been made so."

As suddenly as it had flared up, the anger left him. He was holding her, looking into those unflinching dark eyes, and the other feelings she stirred in him came flooding in to take the place of anger. He wanted heat, not the bitter heat of rage that dried the heart and left the taste of ashes in the mouth, but the sweet melting heat he knew he could find in Susannah Bowen.

Her eyes told him she sensed his change in mood, and she stiffened slightly in his arms.

He released her and looked away. "At least, Mrs. Bowen, you can't accuse me of being cold."

"I'm sorry. I know nothing of your . . . past. I should not let gossip guide my judgment of you."

"My past is war, rage, revenge. I thought I was done with it when my father died, but whoever the card thief is, he wants to keep it going." He paused. Her eyes were serious now, full of the shadows of some pain. "I could use your help," he said.

"My lord, I will never help you to endanger my cousin."

"Then I shall have to call upon your aunt, Mrs. Bowen. Good day."

Kirby started at the sound of light footsteps and rose from his crouched position between a column and the iron railing of a neighboring house. He ducked again. It was not Miss Lacy but her cousin leaving the house and striding off purposefully. Sharp disappointment mastered him for a moment so that he did not hear a second set of footsteps until they hesitated. He raised his head and looked at the Lacy house again. There she was just as they'd agreed at the foot of the steps, in a blue pelisse. He felt giddy with relief and took a deep, steadying breath before he left his hiding place and strolled her way.

She saw him, broke into a wide smile, and hurried to meet him. He contented himself with taking her hand, instead of kissing her in the street, but there was great pleasure in holding that trusting hand, keeping it warm in his.

"Come," he said, tugging her along.

She complied, readily falling into step with him, silent until they turned the first corner.

"Did you stay on at the ball?" she asked.

"You danced with my father," he said.

"Once. I had to."

"Is he one of your suitors?"

"No. He's not on Papa's list, and I wouldn't choose him anyway."

"He's very rich."

"Papa is too."

"He has a title."

"Don't you?" There was nothing she would not ask.

He didn't answer. He was struck by the way the golden curls under her bonnet framed her face.

"I didn't give you away, you know," she confided. "I wouldn't. Susannah thinks I have no discretion at all, but no one knows I've seen you in town."

He smiled at that. "Good."

He led her south and east until the street opened on a square with trees in bud overhead and green shoots underfoot. She frowned. "I would like to know why I mustn't tell anyone about you. Why are you hiding? Doesn't your father acknowledge you?"

"My father doesn't know I exist."

She stopped abruptly. "How can your father not know about you?"

He pulled her onward toward a bench still wet from the night's rain and spread his coat on it. "He abandoned my mother before I was born," he told her, indicating with a gesture that she should sit. Instead she began to pace. He shrugged and sat down to watch.

"Why?"

"I asked that question, too. How any man could leave her . . . She said it was because his father, the old marquess, objected, and that they were forced apart. She was always sure he would come back to her, but he didn't. He came to London and made his fortune and lived well, while she . . . toiled for others."

"He must have been very young then," Miss Lacy said, stopping in front of him.

Kirby glanced up at her. She was right, of course, he realized. He never thought of his father as young, but his parents had married in January of '97, and he had been born in September of that year. So his father must have been seventeen when he, Kirby, was born.

"Will you ever tell him who you are?" she asked.

"I have to. I promised my mother I would, but not until I'm ready."

"You're not ready then?"

"No, I . . . have more to do."

"What?"

"The things he did. My mother kept note of them, and I want to do them, to show him who I am."

"Will that be soon?"

"This spring, you mean? Yes."

"I'm glad."

"That doesn't mean I'll be able to call on you at your mother's."

"Why not?"

He stood and picked up his coat, shaking the moisture from it. He had not meant to tell her as much as he had. "Listen, this is just a temporary friendship."

She stopped pacing and stared at him. "What do you mean?"

"Like Odysseus and Nausikaa."

"Who?"

"He was a Greek king, who lost his way and washed ashore on an island. The princess Nausikaa helped him. And then, he had to go on."

Her expression was decidedly cool. "I liked being Romeo and Juliet better."

"Maybe," he said, laughing, "but they came to a tragic end. You wouldn't want that."

"No," she said, and turned and began walking determinedly back the way they had come.

"Wait," he called.

She did not answer, but reached the gate to the square and stopped to fiddle with the latch. He caught up with her and held the gate closed with his foot.

"You have your plans. I have mine. Can't we be friends for now?"

"You haven't even told me your name," she said. Her chin was high, but there was a bright tear on her cheek.

"If I tell you my name, can we talk again?"

"Last night you wanted to kiss me," she said.

She turned slowly, and he felt his stomach take a swooping dive like a swallow. "That hasn't changed," he admitted, looking into those blue eyes.

"Your name?" she demanded.

"Kirby," he said.

13

❧❧❧

The evening of the opening subscription ball of the season, the ladies of the Lacy household descended her ladyship's stairs, conscious of the late hour and the patronesses' insistence on timely arrival.

"Susannah, you promised you would not wear a cap tonight," remarked Evelina somewhat crossly.

"I promised I would not wear a cornette, Aunt. No one will remark on this sort of cap at all, and I shall remain among the chaperones all night," Susannah replied.

"It's Almack's, dear. You must wear feathers. I'm certain I have some that would look well with that lavender gown."

"No thank you, Aunt."

"Think of Juliet, dear. She mustn't be thought a dowd," Evelina pleaded.

"Oh well, Mama, I don't suppose it really matters, does it?" Juliet said.

They had come halfway down the last flight of steps. Chettle was beaming up at his mistress from the entry.

"Has the carriage been brought round, Chettle?" she asked.

"Yesh, mi . . . la . . . dy," he said.

He stepped back, bowed with sweeping formality, and crumpled in an undignified heap upon the marble squares of the entry.

"Ooooh," Evelina wailed.

Two footmen rushed to the fallen man's side. One pulled the bell rope. Evelina scurried to Chettle and went down on her knees on the marble tiles. A maid poked her head into the entry, took one wide-eyed look at the scene, and dashed off through the door to the kitchens.

"Poor dear man," Evelina said to the footmen. "How is his head? I distinctly heard his head crack against the tiles."

"Felt nothing, ma'am," said one of them. "Fair foxed he is."

"Not again," cried Evelina. "Mrs. Chettle will be in a taking."

Susannah and Juliet had reached the bottom of the stairs, and from where they stood, the smell of sherry was unmistakable.

Mrs. Chettle strode into the entry with a swish of bombazine, looking very stern. She cast an offended glance over her husband's prostrate form and lifted Evelina to her feet. "Now, my lady," she said. "You mustn't trouble yourself about this foolish old man." She turned to the footmen. "Thomas and James, you will convey Mr. Chettle to his bed."

The two footmen grasped Chettle's shoulders and feet and lifted him off the floor. Chettle groaned.

"He lives," breathed Evelina.

Mrs. Chettle turned back to her mistress. "There my lady, Chettle is alive, and you may take Miss Juliet and Mrs. Bowen to Almack's just as you planned."

"But we must send for a doctor. I must see that Chettle has received no injury to the skull," Evelina protested.

"You go ahead, Mama," said Juliet. "We don't have to go to Almack's tonight."

Juliet's suggestion brought all movement in the entry to a halt and drew every eye but Chettle's to her.

"Not go to Almack's!" Evelina cried, dropping her air of trembling helplessness. "My dear, you don't mean it. You must be seen there. Your papa may think it a foolish extravagance to attend, but if you want anyone other than Brentwood, you must go."

Juliet shrugged. "If you say so, Mama."

"Wait here," said Evelina in more commanding tones. "I won't be but a minute. I must see Chettle comfortable. Then to Almack's. Brummell's all to pieces and who knows what they will be saying about Byron."

The footmen bearing Chettle lurched off, followed by Evelina and Mrs. Chettle, debating the wisdom of sending for a doctor. Juliet yawned and looked about as if expecting a comfortable sofa to present itself for her convenience. Susannah stole a glance at her cousin. This was not the girl who a fortnight earlier had wanted scores of suitors. Susannah had not yet confronted her cousin with Lord Warne's suspicions, but now she studied Juliet closely.

The girl was gazing into a tall mirror, her head tilted to the left, staring absently at her own image. Her golden hair was fashioned in curls about her face. Under her evening cloak, she wore a simple white gown, its dainty sleeves dotted with pearls, its filmy skirts ending in a lace border above the white kid slippers.

"Juliet," Susannah began, "have you seen that highwayman again? Here in London?"

The girl leaned forward, apparently intent on arranging the curls that framed her face. "What makes you think I have?" she asked.

"He was at the Royston ball," Susannah stated flatly.

"Oh?"

"He left his card, that is, Lord Warne's card."

"With you?" Juliet cast her a quick glance.

"No. I don't know with whom he left it, but it came into Lord Warne's hands, and he is not pleased."

Juliet looked down, pulling at the pink tulips in a vase on a half-moon table. "I suppose he isn't, but what has that to do with me?"

Susannah counseled herself to patience. "Nothing, of course, if you neither see this person nor encourage his folly."

"Folly?"

"What else are we to call his actions? Going about London leaving the cards of a man of title and power? What good can come of such a prank?" Susannah did not want to reveal that the cards were stolen.

Juliet turned toward Susannah. "But you don't know his reasons."

Susannah started. "You *have* seen him. You were with him in the garden at the Roystons'. Juliet, you must not take such chances with your reputation. You will be ruined."

"Ruined? I'm not worried about *that*."

"But you must be. Even the least misstep and you may be the object of malicious gossip."

"I don't care," said Juliet stubbornly. "I won't end up like you, Susannah. I want something to happen in my life."

Susannah thought of the truth, the sad, ugly, terrible truth. If she told it, would it help Juliet? "I

must not be your model then. Look how happy the
princess is with Saxe-Coburg. She seems to have
chosen very well from among the ranks of young
men suitable to her station."

"*Young* men," Juliet said pointedly. "All Papa's
choices are old."

"But your mother's choices are young enough,
and perhaps you will meet someone at Almack's
whom we can add to your father's list."

"I don't want anyone from a list. I want someone . . ." Juliet broke off with a considering look.

"You want someone dangerous," said Susannah.

"Yes." Juliet's eyes opened wide. "You do understand."

Oh yes. Susannah understood. *They won't approve
of me, you know,* Randolph Price had confided in her,
and she had felt privileged to share his conspirato-
rial glance. He had praised her for every deception
that had won them a stolen moment here and there,
encouraging her to take greater and greater risks,
until she had put herself in his hands. Oh yes, she
knew the attractions of danger. To Juliet, she said,
"You must not see the highwayman again."

Just then Evelina returned. "Come girls. I don't
mean for Ann Trentfield to have all the *on dits*."

They presented their tickets at the door, and Susannah felt her stomach knot. The place had hardly
changed in ten years, but she was no longer an
unsullied miss. She had a sudden vision of the
patronesses discovering her unworthiness and driving her from the rooms. Then as they surrendered
their cloaks to an attendant, she laughed at herself to think that she would be accorded the least
notice among the glittering company. Her ruin was
long forgotten. Her long-sleeved lavender gown
was plain, and, of course, her cap marked her as
a chaperone.

She entered with at least outward calm until she saw Lord Warne. He was dressed in the prescribed manner in white satin knee breeches and black coat, and he looked indifferent as ever to the opinion of society. They were acknowledged adversaries now, but his gaze met hers, recalling the heated moment in the park when he had been about to kiss her again. She fanned her cheeks and looked away.

Evelina spotted Mrs. Trentfield and led them into the room, greeting acquaintances as they passed.

Then Juliet said, "Susannah, there's a young man staring at you."

"You must be mistaken," Susannah replied. "Everyone is looking at you."

"Susannah, I am quite serious. This man is looking at you."

Susannah turned. "Where?"

"There," said Juliet. "With the Grangerfords."

Susannah followed her cousin's gaze. A very young gentleman with fine expressive eyes and a head of dark curls was looking at her with a mixture of hope and inquiry.

She felt her fingers close tightly around her fan. She knew that face though she had not seen it for ten years. Time had altered her youngest brother Henry in the nicest way. He had been a round-faced boy of twelve when she had last seen him. Now he had a firm jaw and lean cheeks with no lessening of the brightness of his eyes. It was plain that he thought he recognized her, and just as plain that he did not know what to do about it. Whatever her brothers had been told about her disgrace, they could not have a good opinion of her character. He must wonder that she dared to enter the holy of holies.

"He must think me an oddity," she said to Juliet,

striving for a light tone. She looked about for Evelina and met Ann Trentfield's curious gaze. Susannah turned away and directed Juliet to the side of the room where their acquaintances had gathered. Garrett, Newbury, and Lord Eastham were all there, with other gentlemen eager to be presented to Miss Lacy. But when Juliet went off to dance a quadrille with Mr. Newbury, Susannah felt conspicuously alone. She shook off the feeling that her brother was watching her and joined a group of matrons and young ladies around Evelina.

"Your girl seems to be faring well, Evie," suggested Mrs. Trentfield.

"Very well," said Evelina. "So lovely tonight and so many beaux."

"But is anyone likely to come up to scratch?" Mrs. Trentfield asked.

"Well, it is early yet, but I'm sure someone will. The most promising thing is that Lord Warne approached me only yesterday. He wants to arrange a small party for Vauxhall. His title is high, to be sure, but then he *has* taken an interest in the girl since her arrival."

"Since you spread that silly story about a highwayman with the man's card," said Mrs. Trentfield. "She's not his usual style, you know."

"I'm sure she's lovely enough, and if he means to marry, he will be conscious of his name and position and choose a girl of good birth."

"She certainly will have pin money if she lands him, but won't she be rather cowed by the Iron Lord?" Ann raised one sleek brow. "His carnal appetite is said to be as fierce as Byron's."

"Is it true, Ann, that Byron has established Mrs.

Mardyn in the house?" asked Mrs. Chaworth-Musters.

"Oh I think it's worse than that," replied Ann. "You have heard what Lady B. told Mrs. Beecher-Stowe?"

Evelina protested that she had not and had to be informed. "Oh the unnaturalness of it," she exclaimed, her blue eyes wide. "And Mrs. Leigh is in his house too?"

"The man apparently requires a harem," said Mrs. Chaworth-Musters. "He'll be better served in the East should he return there."

"He should have married me," offered Miss Mercer Elphinstone, a bright-eyed, red-haired flirt that Susannah had observed at the Shalford ball. "He wants managing," she said boldly and with the obvious assurance that she could supply this lack in Lord Byron's life.

"He wants," said Susannah, "respect and sympathy, and some privacy in which to sort out his differences with his wife."

The little crowd of women turned to her, their faces expressing surprise as if a chair had spoken. Mrs. Trentfield spoke for them all. "Byron's ruined himself. And the censure he's earned is ruin's inevitable reward."

"He has forfeited all claim to feminine sympathy," Mrs. Chaworth-Musters added.

"He shall have mine," Susannah said quietly. Byron's heroes had expressed the pain of remorse so forcefully, she could not think of him without compassion or imagine that he was not suffering as much as his wife.

"Good evening, ladies," said Lord Warne. He was standing unexpectedly near, his gaze fixed on

Susannah. He greeted each of the ladies in turn. Then he said, "Mrs. Bowen, I believe you promised me the first waltz."

Nothing could have prevented Susannah from showing her astonishment, but she dipped into a curtsy and accepted his arm.

"This is absurd," she said when she recovered her presence of mind. They were about to take their place upon the floor, and the glances of others were obvious. "You must excuse me," she whispered. "We will be the subject of talk."

"Then we'll spare Byron. You were defending him just now, weren't you?"

"Yes, but . . . How did you know?"

He clasped her right hand and took hold of her waist, and the question went out of her mind. "I can't," she said. "I can't dance with . . . a cap." She reached up with her left hand to touch the bit of muslin and lace perched on her head.

He drew her a little closer, his eyes fixed on hers. "I would remove it, but I think that would occasion more talk than you can bear. It will not impede your steps. Only smile and look on me as a friend, and we will carry this off."

"Are you utterly indifferent to opinion?"

"Utterly," he said. A slow smile transformed his face, lighting his eyes, making the Iron Lord vanish. "Dance with me, Susannah Bowen," he urged.

"I can't," she protested, but the musicians struck the opening notes, and the motion of others required that they, too, move. And as she did so, the music freed her steps from caution.

"You can," Warne whispered in her ear.

"Susannah's dancing," Juliet observed to her mother a few minutes later.

"And everyone is watching," Evelina replied. "It is that ridiculous cap the girl insists upon wearing."

"I don't think so, Mama," Juliet replied thoughtfully. "It is how lovely she is. I never noticed before."

At the end of their waltz, Lord Warne insisted that they take a turn about the rooms before he would relinquish her company. Each moment made Susannah more conscious of the notice their dance had drawn.

"Smile," he ordered. "Even I can't kiss you here."

"Are you doing this to embarrass me?"

"No," he said with some heat. "May I not dance with the only woman in the room who is not weighing my merits as a matrimonial prospect."

"You have *other* merits?" she said.

"Touché," he said. "I'm well served for my conceit. In any case I will dance with all the others in your party starting with that cat Ann Trentfield if you think the gossips must be appeased." With that he surrendered her to the group around Juliet.

Susannah was attempting to compose her disordered senses when she heard her name and froze. It was Henry, his voice not unlike her father's, the voice that had reviled her yet had been missed.

"Susannah Lacy?"

"Once," she said. "Now, Susannah Bowen."

"I thought so when I first saw you," he said. "But I . . . couldn't be sure until you danced just now. Then I remembered. You were such a good dancer. Young as I was then, I remember. You always danced beautifully."

Several people were near enough to hear this exchange. Juliet was looking at her with frank interest, and Ann Trentfield's eyes were upon her again.

When Susannah remained silent, he said, "I'm Henry, your brother. You do remember me, don't you?"

Susannah looked at the earnest, hopeful face, and yielded. He had been but a boy. He had not cast her off. "Yes," she said. "I do."

"Fancy our meeting here," he continued. "I would never have looked for you here. . . . That is I didn't know you'd come to town, thought you were somewhere in the country."

"Let me present you to Miss Lacy, our cousin. I've come with her for the season."

Juliet offered her hand and smiled at her newly met cousin.

"And your husband?" her brother asked.

"Bowen is dead," Susannah replied tightly.

"Oh, of course," said her brother. "Let me present you to the Grangerfords."

There followed a cold, formal exchange that left Susannah feeling that her poor brother had blundered if he hoped to impress Miss Grangerford's family with his town polish. Mrs. Grangerford clearly had no relish for introductions to mere chaperones. Her glance took in Susannah's cap with icy disdain.

"May I call on you?" her brother asked in parting.

"Of course," Susannah replied.

It was Mrs. Trentfield who claimed the *on dit* of the evening in conversation with her friend Mrs. Chaworth-Musters.

"Evelina is so blind. That companion of her daughter's is hot enough under her cap and fichu. You may be sure Warne's onto her."

"An improper widow?"

"Very. The name Bowen threw me at first, but of course, she was Susannah Lacy before. We came out in the same season. I remembered when I saw her dance. She was mad for a penniless officer. The name will come back to me, not Bowen, I'm sure."

"Is she the one who ran off? After the Ravenswood ball?"

"Yes, but I didn't ever hear that she'd married."

"Not Price. That was the fellow she ran off with. He threw up a dozen skirts that spring."

"I wonder where she got Bowen? Her brother didn't seem to realize she'd married. You would think the family would acknowledge her if she had married."

14

Henry Lacy called on his sister the day after their meeting at Almack's. He brought his friend Edward Noakes, with whom he shared rooms near Gray's Inn, where the two were studying the law. They were welcomed indifferently by Evelina and allowed to sit apart from her other callers. After the formalities had passed, a question from Susannah about the nature of their studies elicited an easy flow of talk from the two young men. Upon the arrival of another set of callers, Juliet left the fashionable circle around her mother and drifted over to the sunny corner where Susannah and her guests sat.

"The thing is," said Henry, "the law is the great instrument for moral good. It embodies our aspirations for justice."

"But laws just tell us what we can't do, don't they?" Juliet asked, speaking up for the first time.

"Well," Henry replied frowning, "there are a number of laws that prohibit this and that . . ."

"Thousands," interjected Ned.

Henry glared at his friend. "But even those laws are teaching us virtue—the virtue of forbearance."

"Prudence, at any rate," suggested Ned dryly.

"I say forbearance," insisted Henry with a flash of his fine brown eyes. "The law teaches us a decent respect for others by requiring that we not act on our impulses of selfishness, malice, or revenge."

Ned applauded. "Can't you just hear how he'll be in court?" he asked, and Henry reddened.

"I am inclined to oratory," he confessed in lowered tones.

"Your brother," said Ned to Susannah, "sees the law as a golden city, whereas I see it as a garden overrun with weeds."

"And yet you share lodgings?" Susannah teased. She could see how close a friendship this was and knew her brother could not find a like companionship with Richard.

Ned laughed. "Henry may have his head in the clouds about the law, but nobody likes a good mill quite as much as he does."

"A mill?" asked Juliet. "You like boxing, Mr. Lacy?"

A passionate spark lit Henry's dark eyes again. "Going to see a mill this Sunday at Hill's. The Sinister Scot against Beecham the Bruiser. Tom Cribb himself will be there. Should be quite a match," Henry said.

"We saw the Bruiser last month," Ned Noakes explained. "He's got fists the size of melons, and he's immovable as an oak."

"What about the other gentleman?" Juliet asked.

"Haven't seen the Scot, yet," Henry told her. "He's a young fellow, brought up by Hill. Supposed to have a wicked left."

"Will there be any ladies there?" Juliet asked.

The two young men gaped at her. "Ladies," said Ned recovering first, "should never attend a mill."

"Is that a *law*, Mr. Noakes?" asked Juliet.

"It should be," Ned replied heatedly.

"Well, I'd like to know why," said Juliet.

Ned began to tell her, and Henry turned to

Susannah. "I hope I did right in coming here, Susannah," he said. "Last night, well, last night you did not look pleased to acknowledge me. I have been a poor excuse for a brother to be so caught up in making my own way in life and not to think about what became of you or how you were faring. I never even heard you had married or anything," he concluded.

Susannah studied her hands folded in her lap. She had not minded concealing the truth in the country. No one remarked her, and to have *Mrs.* before her name merely meant she could go about her duties undisturbed. Nor had she minded her deception in London. Any scandal attached to her would only harm Juliet. But in the face of her brother's kindness she suddenly wanted only truth. It would hurt him with the Miss Grangerfords of society if he were kind to an erring sister, but she looked up to find him regarding her with that hopeful gaze and could not bear to lose his friendship so soon. "It was good of you to call, Henry. I am grateful and glad to see you getting on so well." Conscience made her ask, "Won't Richard object?"

Henry frowned. "I suppose he will. He's rather stiff that way, likes me to be sure everyone I meet is well-connected. He can't even like Ned, but we need not tell Richard we're friends."

"I would not want you to quarrel with him on my account, Henry," Susannah said. "But I shall always be glad to see you."

"You must rely on me," he told her, casting a glance at Evelina. "If you need someone on your side in a fix."

Kirby's seconds pressed a cold sponge to the cut above his right eye. His ribs ached with every breath. He let his lids close and shut out the noise and confusion of the crowd and the worried faces of the friends who'd bet on him. The fight had been grim. The Bruiser had a stolid cunning and was not easily moved or tricked. Kirby's speed had saved him from the man's blows, but his own punches might have fallen on stone for all their effect upon his opponent. He was like a gnat trying to worry a bull.

He studied his opponent again, remembering that Hill's word on the Bruiser was that the man had never had to go the distance. He'd always brought his rival down in the first rounds. Those heavy fists were first a threat, then a liability. In the early rounds they had been swinging for Kirby's head, and had just one of them caught him on the ear or the jaw, he'd have been felled. In the last round the huge fists had been catching him in the ribs, as if the Bruiser didn't have the strength to lift them higher. Kirby pictured the man's shifts and feints. What was the Bruiser covering?

When the seconds finished in his corner, he stood and moved toward the mark. The crowd shouted its impatience. The Bruiser advanced with slow, heavy steps, and Kirby mimicked him step for step, trying to feel with his own body the man's weariness, his uncertain balance. There was an exchange of blows and then a clinch, with the Bruiser resting his bulk on Kirby. The referee parted them, and then the Bruiser ducked to avoid Kirby's right. The duck was a bit too heavy, too slow, leaving an opening for Kirby's left. He danced right, drawing the big man after him, fending off heavy blows. Then he tried the right feint again, brought the answering duck, and let fly with a driving left that met the Bruiser's chin just as the man lowered it.

The blow lifted him, and he fell back, shoulders and head hitting the canvas.

The crowd went still for a moment then erupted into cries as the referee made the count. The Bruiser heaved himself up to his knees, shaking his head, flinging sweat. Then he rose unsteadily to his feet. There was the half-minute rest period. Then the big man lunged at Kirby and almost went down again from his own momentum. The ropes caught him, and he came back to the center of the ring, swinging madly. It was Kirby's turn to duck, and he knew an instant of blackness when one of the huge fists caught him a glancing blow on the side of the head.

The crowd was yelling wildly now. The Bruiser was spending all in a last burst of energy. Kirby would have to wait for the flailing fists to slow down. He kept moving, a light dance that drew the man's heavy steps after him, dodging the blows with the bob and weave of his upper body, waiting, waiting. The Bruiser hit the ropes again, righted himself, and staggered back into the ring, holding his fists below a proper fighting stance. Kirby moved in. There came the downswing of the heavy head in response to his right feint. His left fist flashed up and caught the Bruiser square in the face. There was a snap like a dried limb breaking from a tree, and the Bruiser simply crumpled to the mat.

The ring filled with onlookers, who clapped Kirby on the back and shouted in his ears. Hill held Kirby's arm aloft in the traditional sign of victory. Then he was lifted up on the shoulders of Garrett and others and borne out of the ring.

His friends left him in the changing room and went off to collect on their bets. Hill and his seconds bustled about sponging him down, offering water, fussing over his damaged hands, Hill criticizing every move of the fight. Kirby heard it all as if from a great distance. He had done it. He had won in the ring just as his father had beaten Lockyer, the Guardsman, years before. When he was dressed, he was led back to the hall to receive the purse.

Burly Tom Cribb himself made the presentation. "You've got bottom, lad," he said. He handed Kirby a leather pouch, heavy with coin. Kirby took the prize and held it up for all to see. Then he was surrounded by friends and strangers who wanted to relive the fight blow by blow and buy him a drink. Garrett was shouting, "The Scot, the Scot." Someone put a tankard in Kirby's free hand. He raised it to his friends and took a deep draft. Hill clapped him on the back and shoved him into the crowd.

Several rounds later Hill returned and pulled Kirby over to the champion's table. Cribb asked Hill a dozen questions about Kirby's skills and experience, then he wanted to know, "Have you got a backer for the lad?"

Kirby shook his head, clearing it of the ale. "I've got my own backer," he said. "I'd like the purse sent round to him, if you don't mind, Mr. Cribb." He laid one of his father's cards on the table. Cribb took it, and cast Kirby a shrewd glance. "What's your name, lad?"

Kirby gave the name he'd been using at Hill's. Cribb looked doubtful. He signalled to one of his men. "Teague, deliver this to his lordship tonight."

It was a test, but Kirby kept his gaze steady under Cribb's.

"Save some for yourself, boy," Hill advised, gesturing at the purse.

Kirby opened the leather pouch and retrieved a handful of coins before he handed his prize over to the messenger. "With the card," he insisted. Cribb gave the card to his man, and the messenger set off.

"Well, then, Hill," he said. "I think we can do something with this one." The two men returned to their talk of future fights, and Kirby considered how much time he had to make an escape.

Warne returned from yet another ball where Susannah Bowen had disturbed his peace. He retired to his library, settled himself in a chair before the fire, and swirled the bit of brandy in his glass. She definitely clouded his mind. Her discreet presence among the chaperones had made him lose his train of thought more than once. The start of a waltz had set him moving toward her when he was pledged to another. He remembered too well their kiss in the park, their dance at Almack's, recollections that made him restless in a way that neither work nor running could settle.

She thought him ruthless and cold and willing to destroy anyone to achieve his ends, and he could not deny that he had become so, that he was not the boy who had loved and married Ellen Kirby. He wanted to protest that there was a warmer side to his nature, that he could laugh and dance and perhaps love. Let him capture this thief, and he would prove it.

A knock on the library door interrupted these reflections. Pedrick entered with his usual discretion, announcing, "A messenger, sir. The man insists on seeing you."

"At this hour?" Warne asked, wondering that his butler had not summarily dismissed the caller.

"He presented this card, sir," said Pedrick, handing it over.

Warne was on his feet instantly. He slammed the brandy down on a side table. "Who is he?"

"A Mr. Teague. I'd say a pugilist, sir."

Warne strode past his astonished butler. In the entry he found a hulk of a man with a flattened nose and a loud waistcoat. At the sound of Warne's steps, the fellow looked around.

"Beggin' your lordship's pardon," he said. "But Mr. Cribb says you're the backer to tonight's boy. Wanted you to have the purse." The man held out a leather pouch sagging with the weight of coin.

Warne took the purse. "Mr. Teague, pardon me, you say this purse was won tonight? Where?"

"At Hill's, my lord. Just about an hour ago. Fine fight it was, too."

"The winner sends me this purse and this card?"

Teague nodded.

It made no sense that the thief would send him prize money, but he had no time to puzzle out the mystery. "Did you come in a hack, Teague? Is it waiting?"

The old fighter nodded.

"Then I'd like to join you. I'd like to shake this fellow's hand."

Teague's eyes opened wide at the suggestion. "It'd be an honor, your lordship, I'm sure."

By the time they reached Hill's establishment in Stanhope Street, Warne knew the young boxer had to be the man behind the other appearances of his card as well. The name Teague gave meant nothing to Warne, but all the other details fit too well.

As they pulled up opposite the place, Warne questioned Teague about a back entrance and was assured that it was locked during a match to keep

the flash-coves out. Warne had the jarvey position
the hack on the opposite side of the street, where he
could view the swinging front doors. He remained
in the hack. If the thief had not anticipated Warne's
being at home to receive the purse, he might be in
the place yet, and easily trapped or foolish enough
to bolt.

Warne did not risk taking Teague into his confidence. He simply asked Teague to report the delivery of the purse and to return to the hack if the
young man had left.

Kirby saw the old fighter return. Perhaps an hour
had slipped by after all. Something in Teague's
manner bothered him. The man was looking about.
Their gazes met, and Teague gave a nod as if satisfied on some point. Kirby glanced at the swinging
doors. No sign of anyone there and only the darkness of the street beyond. Surely his father would
not come here. He set down his tankard, regretting
that he'd let thirst and fellowship get the better of
him. He ought to have made his escape an hour
ago. His knuckles were swollen, the bruises on his
ribs ached in spite of the ale's effect. He thought
fleetingly of the back door, but suspected it was
still locked on account of the match.

The front door was the only means of escape. He
put his arm around Garrett's shoulder, leaned close,
and whispered the name of a place of which Garrett
was said to be fond. Garrett turned and a slow, wicked grin lighted his face. He rose to his feet and gave
a shout like a battle cry. Newbury, Eastham, and
several others looked his way, and in a minute all
were gathering coats and hats. Eastham flung a jin-
gle of silver at the tapman, and the group began to
jostle its way to the swinging doors. Kirby put on
his hat, his father's hat, at an angle that matched

his friends'. He had no plan but Odysseus's plan, to remain concealed by the group until they reached a turning. If someone waited in the dark, Kirby would watch for the man to make a move, then he would break and run.

The quarter-hour bell sounded from a nearby church tower. Teague had not returned. Warne doffed his hat, shed his coat, and descended from the hack. The jarvey protested, and Warne tossed him another coin. He crossed the street and stood flush against the outer wall of Hill's in the shadow of an overhanging upper story.

Just then, a group of young gentlemen burst through the doors, clumsy with drink, staggering, swearing, laughing.

"Hey ho," said one of the group, coming to a swaying halt. "There's a hack."

"What do we want with a hack, Garrett? There's eight of us. Come on. It's not far to Roxy's."

"Right," said the first gentleman. He spun on his heel, nearly tripped, and lurched after his companions.

Silently, Warne drew up behind the group. Garrett had been at the Royston ball, and the thief might have used him as an entré. He scanned the backs of the heads in front of him, but they all looked much the same.

They reached the first corner, and one of the young men groaned. "Going to cast up my accounts," he proclaimed. His fellows giggled. Then Warne saw a hatless, coatless figure stumble around the turning. The next moment he heard purposeful steps running away. With a cry he lunged through the young men and dashed after the runner.

The thief's ploy had given him yards on Warne,

but a broad straight street lay before them with no corners before the distant thoroughfare of Drury Lane. Warne lengthened his stride and pushed himself. They were well matched for height and speed, and Warne knew the thief's head start was just the edge that had to be overcome. He gained a yard, and the thief brushed a stack of crates standing outside a shop, sending their contents tumbling into the road, forcing Warne to check and swerve.

He closed the gap again, could hear the breathing of his adversary. Drury Lane was just ahead, choked with carriages lined up awaiting theatre goers. He stretched out his arm. They burst into the lane. The thief angled right and dove between the horses of one carriage and the rear of another. The startled animals shied, and the driver cursed and wrestled with his team.

Warne sidestepped to the next opening in the line and plunged through. He saw the thief roll under a carriage further down the line, and when he broke through again, the man was gone.

Kirby figured he had lost his father somewhere around the theatre, but he didn't stop running until he'd passed Covent Garden. Then he stopped and cast up his accounts on a pile of refuse against a wall. For several long minutes he could not decide whether it was more necessary to breathe or to wretch. Then he picked himself up and headed back to his rooms. Lord, his father was fast.

15

Warne made an afternoon call upon the Lacy household in order to fix the date for the proposed party to Vauxhall Gardens. He was fortunate to find the ladies alone in the blue and gold drawing room, a circumstance which no doubt accounted for Lady Lacy's welcoming effusions, Miss Lacy's listlessness, and a slight stiffening of Mrs. Bowen's back. He accepted a seat at his hostess's right, from which he could observe the neat, steady movements of Mrs. Bowen's hand as she set stitches in a bit of linen.

Lady Lacy professed herself delighted with the Vauxhall scheme. "How clever of you, Warne, to have procured a box just after the royal wedding. They say the world will be there."

Warne saw Mrs. Bowen's hand falter. Her gaze flew up to his, and he met it with a steady look of his own. She had to know he could not bend in this. He had been inches from catching the thief and would not be denied again.

"Juliet, dear," Lady Lacy continued. "What a treat for you. Your first time to the gardens. The program is bound to be extravagant."

"It will be," Warne agreed. "I understand the cascade is to be altered to honor the royal couple. Of course, the fireworks will be extended."

Juliet Lacy stirred at that. "It's a public garden, isn't it, Lord Warne?" she asked, not meeting his eye, but plucking at the folds of her skirt.

"It is, Miss Lacy," he replied. "Thieves and Cyprians frequent the place, but I assure you in the company of your family and friends and with a private supper box, our party will be quite safe from any unwanted attentions." He felt Mrs. Bowen's gaze, but did not turn.

"Ma'am," he said to Lady Lacy, "that brings me to the point of my call. I thought you might advise me as to which of your acquaintances I should include in the party."

"Oh how kind, of course, let me think."

Susannah looked at her flustered aunt. Evelina was naming her favorite companions one by one. How clever the Iron Lord was being. Flattered and surrounded by friends of her own choosing, Evelina would be absorbed in the pleasures of Vauxhall and pay no heed to Juliet at all. What, Susannah wondered, did Warne mean to do with her to see that she, too, relaxed her chaperone's guard? And how did he plan to alert the young highwayman of his plans? Would he put a notice in the papers? Her reflections were interrupted when she realized the others were staring at her.

"I beg your pardon," she said.

"Susannah," Juliet said, "I think you should invite someone."

Susannah could see that Evelina did not share her daughter's view. "Who?" she asked.

"Well, your brother, of course, and his friend," Juliet suggested.

"Thank you, Juliet," Susannah said, recovering from the surprise of being noticed and considered. She looked at Warne. He was frowning, and it was plain he had not anticipated Juliet's request. "I would love to have Henry and Ned included, if Lord Warne does not mind."

Lord Warne made no objections. The guest list was decided upon, and the gentleman stood to take his leave. Just then Chettle announced new callers, and Evelina greeted them. A single stride brought Warne to Susannah, so near her skirts might brush his boots. With a light touch of his fingertips he traced the stitches she had made.

"Have you been to Vauxhall before, Mrs. Bowen?"

She watched the fine strong fingers moving across the little stitches. "Once, long ago," she whispered.

"I hope you will enjoy the evening," he said.

She looked up at that. "I hope so, too, Lord Warne."

Warne returned from his morning run with one black thought on his mind—she had not walked. He understood now that that solitary, free-striding walk was necessary to her, the only unconstrained act she allowed herself each day. And though his mind suggested a dozen impediments to keep her from the park this morning, his heart could think of only one. She would not chance an encounter with him.

He opened the door to the breakfast room and stopped short. There, in his usual place, bent over the spread pages of the morning *Chronicle*, was Neil Bellaby.

His friend looked up, grinning. "Need me I see. You haven't found a bride or a thief, have you?"

"Neither," admitted Warne, stepping forward and extending a hand in greeting. In truth he had forgotten about his search for a bride in the past week. "Don't tell me you've converted that mill to steam already?"

Bellaby explained that the project was going well, so well that he could leave it in the hands of an able assistant while castings were being made of new machine parts. As he listened to Bellaby, Warne toweled off. He settled himself across from his friend with his customary orange and a cup of coffee. He was separating the bright sections of fruit when Bellaby said, "So tell me about the thief."

"He reminds me of me," Warne said. "He's done nearly everything I did to punish my father and at least one thing I wish I'd thought of." He told Bellaby about the thief's stealing his hat and cloak from the Royston ball. "No score left unpaid," he repeated bitterly.

Bellaby was frowning. "But no attacks on your business or finances," he pointed out. "You hurt your father far more with the ready than with petty tricks."

"True," Warne acknowledged. "I thought of that first. I went to Coutts's the day you left and my other bankers as well. They would have informed me of any action of that kind."

"But we have dozens of businesses, hundreds of clients. Have there been no moves against any of them?" Bellaby asked.

"Nothing suspicious."

Bellaby folded up the *Chronicle*. "You still think this fellow is your father's tool?"

"He must be. How I don't know. I've investigated all father's hirelings—Jopp, Reed, Alewood, Bunell. No one is up to anything the least bit suspicious."

"Then the man must be acting alone," Bellaby concluded.

Warne planted his elbows on the table and rested his head in his hands. "I thought of that, but what would drive some stranger to repeat my history? What satisfaction could he gain from embarrassing me?"

"He must not be a stranger. What else do you know about him?"

"I know everything about him except the why. He won the purse at Hill's two nights ago."   Warne lifted his head. He watched the expressions on Bellaby's face as his friend calculated the effort and determination that must have gone into such a victory.

"How did you find out?" his friend asked.

"He sent the purse here, with one of my cards, of course."

Bellaby jumped up. "The devil, you say." He began to pace. "It's not revenge, it's flattery. Imitation . . ." Bellaby waved a hand as if to summon the words he wanted.

" . . . is the sincerest form of flattery," Warne finished.

"Yes, yes! And what does the fellow look like? Hill must have been able to tell you." Bellaby was standing at the window looking out.

"He looks like . . . me, damn it, but . . ."

Bellaby let out a long breath and turned. "The cards say *With my father's compliments*, Warne, not *No score left unpaid*."

"Bellaby, what you're thinking is impossible. If I have a son, he's five or ten, not twenty as this fellow must be."

He sank his head back in his hands. The moment when he knew he would never have a child with Ellen Kirby came back to him. "There's a grave in Scotland, in a village near Dumfries. The girl I married is buried there." He heard Bellaby come back to the table, pull out a chair, and sit down heavily.

"You never told me," Neil whispered.

"I never told anyone. I loved Ellen Kirby from the time we started doing our lessons together under her father's tutelage. He was the vicar in Dovedale. He taught us Latin and Greek and left us to our own devices for part of every afternoon. When I was sixteen, my mother noticed my interest in Ellen and she could not approve. There could be no alliance between our house and the impoverished daughter of an undistinguished cleric. My lessons were ended, would have ended in any case as I was to go off to Oxford. I was forbidden to see Ellen. My father encouraged a young housemaid to seduce me, and she succeeded in educating me and stirring the fires of lust so well that I was soon making love to Ellen secretly. At Christmas my mother discovered us together and reported to my father, who then called me to his library, where he waited with Molly, the maid. He asked me what I thought I was doing. I protested that I loved Ellen and meant to marry her. He reminded me of my absolute dependence on him and pointed out Ellen's father's equal dependence on his good will. He told me I merely had an itch between my legs and that he expected me to satisfy it with Molly and to wait for him to arrange a suitable match for me when I came of age. He knew everything I had done with Molly and suggested I had barely begun to sample the pleasures she could offer. No doubt he was using Molly for his own pleasure. He expected to hear from her by the end of the week that I was a man. But I was already a man, and I would not betray Ellen.

"I went to my mother and got her to plead for me, to let me leave for Oxford at once. I argued that it would separate me from Ellen. Mother got father to agree, and I began to plan an elopement. God, Bellaby, I cost Ellen her life."

His fists closed in futile rage. "We had three days together before he found us. I don't know how he did it. They had no reason to suspect that I had left Oxford or that Ellen was not with her aunt, whom she had said she'd gone to visit. He came with four men and laudanum. They put me in chains. He threatened to rape Ellen in front of me. 'She's the village slut, isn't she,' he said. 'The girl who gives her favors to the highborn sons of the manor. How else does that befuddled father of hers keep his position? That's what they'll say,' he said. 'You've ruined her.'"

Warne stopped for a moment. The hate he had lived with for so many years rose like bile in his throat.

"The chains did not last long. The drug was harder to shake off. I went back as soon as I could, first to the inn where we'd stayed, then to a little village outside of Dumfries. Less than a month had passed, but what I found was that grave. The sexton led me to it. He said she'd died of a fever, like so many others that winter. He gave me the ring I'd put on her finger."

He stopped again, recalling the blackness of that time. He had wanted to kill his father, but on the long numb journey back to Oxford he had decided instead that he would strip his father of everything that mattered to him as he had been stripped of his one joy.

"The bastard," said Bellaby, and Warne heard a world of understanding in the word.

"He was," Warne agreed. He stood and crossed to the window, staring out at the early morning bustle, seeing little.

"You never told anyone, you said."

"Not til now."

"But your mother knew, and that maid. Did your sister know?"

"No." Dullness made him uncomprehending. He had replaced pain with hate, and now he had drained himself of hatred. "What are you getting at, Bellaby?"

"Well, this thief can't be your son, but he wants you to *think* he's your son."

"Why?"

"You're the marquess now. All London must know that you are thinking of marrying. He wants to stake some kind of claim before you leg-shackle yourself and bear a legitimate heir."

Warne turned and stared at his friend.

"Hear me out. The fellow has heard the story. He looks like you. Maybe he's a by-blow of your father's. They must be legion. And he sees a way to profit from his looks."

Warne shook his head. His intuition told him the thief was not acting from a motive as shallow as profit. There was anger and vengeance in these acts, as there had been in his war against his father.

Bellaby shrugged. "Well," he said. "It's a theory. The question is, can you catch the man?"

"I think so," said Warne. "At least I have a plan. Are you willing to help me?"

"Is the regent fat?" Bellaby grinned. "Tell me, what's your plan?"

Warne explained his knowledge of the thief's apparent weakness for Miss Lacy and how he meant to exploit it on their outing to Vauxhall.

"Is Miss Lacy a beauty?" Bellaby asked.

He thought about it. Of course she was, but he had grown accustomed to looking at her dark, slender cousin. "Yes," he said.

"But you're not interested?"

"No." He ran his hands through his hair. "Not in any of this year's girls, I confess. If one is intelligent enough to know what she's about, I can see her weighing the discomforts of my reputation against the size of a marchioness's allowance. The sweeter ones are terrified of me in spite of Maria Sefton's efforts to make me acceptable. Then there's Miss Elphinstone, who had the temerity to tell Byron, and everyone else, that he wanted managing and should have married her. I'd have my hands around her throat inside of a week."

Bellaby laughed. "You've made a rare mull of it then, haven't you? I told you you should find some improper widow and take her to bed."

Bellaby's words stopped him, bringing to mind that remarkable moment in the park when he had found himself kissing Susannah Bowen and wanting to lose himself in her sweetness. Something in his face must have given him away, for Bellaby sat up sharply.

"There is someone," he said worriedly. "Warne, you promised I'd meet anyone you were seriously considering."

"Don't worry, Neil," he said. "Susannah Bowen has as good an opinion of me as I had of my late father."

16

After the cascade, Lord Warne led his guests to the supper box reserved for them. Susannah allowed herself to laugh at something her brother said. The highwayman, if he was there among the masked revelers around them, could not approach Juliet while they ate the famous wafer-thin ham and drank the punch.

She entered the box after the others, but the arrangement of seats put her directly in Lord Warne's view. Every moment his gaze seemed to fall on her, and his nearness in spite of a perfectly respectable distance of some seven or eight feet, caused her a different sort of unease. Her brother's quiet conversation could not keep her from turning at the sound of that other, deeper voice.

For several minutes the talk was of the marvelous cascade and its tribute to the new royal couple. That topic exhausted, Evelina began a discourse on the preparations for Juliet's ball just days away. Susannah's gaze collided with Warne's briefly, and she looked away. Then Ann Trentfield and the Chaworth-Musters strolled by, and Evelina called out to them. Greetings were exchanged, and a place was made for Mrs. Trentfield while her companions sauntered on. Again the wonders

154

of the cascade were remarked until Mrs. Trentfield turned to Susannah.

"But you've been to Vauxhall before, haven't you, Mrs. Bowen?" she asked.

There was a pause. Susannah nodded.

The orchestra began to play dance tunes, and Evelina to complain of the departure in rapid succession of Brummell and Byron. Not even Brentwood's ponderous responses could stem the flow of her ladyship's lament.

At that moment Susannah accepted her brother's invitation to a quadrille. Juliet and Eastham joined them. Susannah was more than glad to leave the confines of the supper box. She could still watch Juliet, and dancing freed some of the unbearable tension of the evening. For a moment she let herself enjoy the lights, the music, the sweetness of the spring air, the freedom to move.

"Is Lord Warne a suitor of Miss Lacy's?" Henry asked.

"Not really," Susannah replied, knowing her brother must be suspicious of the marquess's interest in the Lacys. "He needs Evelina's connections, I think."

"I can't like the way he looks at you, Susannah."

Susannah missed a step and recovered.

"He's offered you no insult, has he?"

"Of course not." Warne did watch her. Her brother's words confirmed it. And there had been that kiss in the park and the waltz at Almack's. As a green girl, she had made much of similar attentions, weaving an illusion of a man's love that had been her ruin. She would not do so again. She shook off thoughts of Warne and glanced around for Juliet. Her cousin and Eastham were just coming down the set, appearing pleased with one another's company. It was

Eastham on whom Susannah now pinned her hopes
of a match for her cousin. His person was unremark-
able but pleasant, his estate had met Uncle Lacy's
approval, and while passionate about his hunting,
Susannah judged him capable of sincere affection.
Susannah allowed herself a small smile. The cottage in Wincanton might be hers after all.

She was just looking for Juliet again at the end of
the set when Lord Warne appeared before her and
solicited her hand. Henry cast her a swift, knowing look, but said nothing to his lordship. With a
slight bow he left them. The other dancers began to
arrange themselves for a waltz, and Warne cocked
an eyebrow, as if daring her to dance with him. She
held her ground, gathering her skirt in one hand.
He stepped up to her and slipped an arm about her
waist, drawing her closer than the dance required
and testing her.

"My lord," she began, and the music started,
sending them into the dizzying whirl she remembered. Within a few turns, he spun her to the edge
of the crowd, and with an abrupt movement, he
drew her away from the others.

"Your cousin is missing," he said.

Kirby said nothing until he had led Juliet where
the distant orchestra faded and the night sounds
of birds, and leaves, and insects humming filled
their ears. He halted beside a stout tree trunk, took
off his coat, and wrapped it around her shoulders.
They had an hour or more until the bell sounded
for the fireworks. Under cover of the noise and
excitement of the display, he would return her to
his father's party. He drew the lapels of the coat
together below her chin and willed himself not to
kiss her right away.

"'Ah, Juliet, if the measure of thy joy be heaped like mine,'" he began.

"Romeo, again," she said, meeting his gaze. "Go on."

"'And that thy skill be more to blazon it, then sweeten with thy breath this neighbor air.'"

"Oh," she said, "but you know I have no skill like that. What does she say?"

He told her.

She repeated, "'But my true love is grown to such excess I cannot sum up half my wealth.'" And he thought he had never heard the line before. He stepped back from her then and shoved his hands in his pockets.

"This has to end you know," he reminded her.

"What has to end?"

"Our . . . friendship, our meetings."

"Why?"

"Because I'm about to finish what I came to London to do."

"And then?" Her voice sounded small.

"I'll leave. I have a passage to America."

"America?" She said it as if he had said the moon. "What will you do there?"

"I'll make my way."

"But you're Lord Warne's son."

"I will throw off my birth. In America no one has a title."

"You could not stay here and be an untitled gentleman?"

"No."

There was a little silence in which a bird, disturbed from its perch, gave a cry and flapped its wings. "Then, we truly must not see one another again." She took the coat from her shoulders and handed it to him.

"You want to end it now?" He hadn't expected that. He had calculated on meeting her several more times. He did not take the coat. If he did not reach out and take it, she could not give it.

"I am no foolish, romantic girl. If you do not love me and wish to marry me, then I don't want to see you again."

"Marry you?" he burst out. He took a couple of steps back from her, stopped, and then strode right up to her again. "I canna' marry you. I have nothing. What a pair we'd be!"

"I have a portion," she said evenly. She was holding the coat folded over her clasped hands.

"Which your father controls," he pointed out. "He could disown you in an hour."

"Well, he wouldn't."

"Well, I willna' be dependent on your money. I've made my way for three years." He had told her how he had worked his way to London with a theatre company.

"Well, if you've made your way, why can't I?"

"Ladies don't."

"Your mother did."

He had to admit she had, but at what cost to her pride and his, to see her toil for that petty, stupid woman. He could not bear it if Juliet Lacy, too, were reduced to such circumstances on account of him. "I don't want that for you."

She took a deep breath. "Then give up your revenge."

"What?"

"Go to your father, and tell him who you are. Let him be a father to you."

"Never." He could not think of anything else to say. Rage and hurt tied his tongue in knots.

She held out the coat again. "I can find my way back," she said.

"No. Ask me something else. I'll do it." He had raised his voice.

She stepped up to him, took his hand, and folded the coat over it. "I have thought about this. Lord Warne does not know about you. He did not deliberately hurt you. But you know about him. You want to hurt him. I'm not sure that's right." Her eyes were solemn. She turned and began to walk away.

"I haven't even kissed you," he called after her.

She stopped. "I know," she answered. "I think it's best if you don't."

"One kiss," he said. He hated to beg, yet he was begging.

She did not turn but only shook her head.

"I can't let you go back alone. I'll walk with you."

She nodded. He came up to her side and saw that she was shivering. Once more he put the coat over her shoulders. They began to walk in silence. His throat hurt, and it was an effort to speak. The noise of the orchestra grew louder and just beyond them through the trees he could see a lighted path where others moved about.

He put a hand on her shoulder and stopped her. She did not look his way. "I must kiss you," he said. He moved around in front of her, taking her other shoulder in his hand, but her face remained stubbornly averted. "For good-bye."

"For good-bye, then," she agreed. She tilted her face up.

He leaned forward, moving as slowly as he could, savoring the feel of her shoulders under his hands, the scent of her, the mingling of their breaths in the cool air, willing the moment to last, to shake her as much as it was shaking him. Their lips met, and she gave him hers in a kiss of piercing sweetness. Then she pulled back.

"Good-bye," she said.

Susannah glanced quickly at the shifting crowd of dancers, the groups strolling along the edge of the colonnade, the party in their supper box. Juliet was nowhere in sight. Lord Warne was striding rapidly away from the dancing area, and Susannah hurried after him. Over her shoulder she could see Lord Eastham and Henry talking to the Miss Phillipses, and next to Evelina, Ann Trentfield, her sharp gaze restlessly scanning the crowd.

"You didn't see Juliet go?" Susannah asked Warne.

"No. She told Eastham she was joining you."

His voice had a sharp edge to it, and her temper flared in response. "This was your doing," she pointed out. "You wanted her here, where her presence might draw your thief, and yet you did not watch her?"

He was looking about, but at that accusation his gaze came back to her. "I took my eyes off her but for a moment. If we find her before the bell rings for the fireworks, you can easily explain her absence."

"We? You expect me to search with *you*?"

"Yes, Mrs. Bowen. Did you want to invite the others to hunt for your cousin?"

She glared at him. "Look for your thief then, Lord Warne. I will look for my cousin."

A thin, copper-haired gentleman dashed up to them, and Warne turned to him.

"Bellaby, did you see them?"

"Saw the girl go through the first arch not two minutes ago with a fellow in a black domino," the gentleman said. He stared at Susannah, giving her an arrested look, as if she were the answer to a puzzling question.

Warne set off for the arch, seizing Susannah's hand and pulling her after him. "Let's find *them*, then," he said.

Beyond the first arch, Bellaby left them, slipping into a band of trees along the lighted walk.

"He lived for five years in Canada, hunting and trapping," Warne explained. "He'll pass through the woods to the end of the park, then work his way back to us. We'll meet somewhere in the middle. We will find them."

The wide, lighted walk stretched away through three more arches. Along its length couples and groups strolled, their laughter and talk making bursts of gaiety in the night air.

"The thief will take her away from the lights and the crowd, as he did at the Royston ball," Warne said. They stepped into the darkness under the trees and began to make their way through the woods. Acres of them, Susannah thought.

In silence they picked their way over roots and around bushes, pausing to listen when they came upon voices in the darkness, circling clearings where a statue or a gazebo stood in moonlight. The music faded, the rustlings of leaves and their own swift steps filled Susannah's ears. There was no sign of Juliet and the highwayman. Other couples talked or embraced or quarreled, but not the pair they sought. She tried to think of Juliet, but the warm joining of her hand with Warne's filled her mind. In that grip she felt the driving energy of the man. She shivered, and Warne stopped.

"You're cold," he whispered, his voice unexpectedly near her ear. His warm breath against her hair made her tremble with a different sensation.

"It's no matter," she said.

He released her hand and removed his coat. Then he draped it around her body. The coat was warm, and he took her by the shoulders. She froze at the contact, unable to move. "Thank you," she said, trying to break the warm, languorous spell of his touch. Juliet was somewhere in the night giving her heart and perhaps her person to a man who could ruin her and leave her with nothing.

Warne's hands fell away from Susannah's shoulders. After a charged moment he led the way again. She concentrated on listening. If their eyes could not spy her cousin, their ears would find her.

When they had been wandering in the wood for the better part of an hour, Susannah stumbled and caught herself by clinging to his hand. He stopped instantly. "Are you all right?" he asked over his shoulder.

"Why weren't you watching her?" she asked. She could not keep the reproach from her voice.

He turned slowly. His hand still gripped hers. A breeze whispered through the trees overhead. "I was watching you."

She suddenly felt weak. "Me?"

"You," he said frankly. "Did you mean to distract me? To protect your cousin and her lover from my wrath?"

"Are you mad?" She pulled back, trying to free her hand from his grip. "I am the one that wants a safe marriage for Juliet. You contrived this evening. You made it a trap for your thief, baited with my cousin."

"Who willingly left the protection of her family for a secret assignation with a highwayman." His hand stilled hers.

"With the man who stole your calling cards." She could not keep the disdain from her voice.

"You have no idea what this thief has done," he said levelly.

"Tell me, then."

He gave a sharp tug on their joined hands, bringing her up against him. His other arm circled her waist and held her pressed to him. "When you tell me why you would consign your daring young cousin to the likes of Brentwood or Eastham. You would never marry such dullness."

Susannah twisted her hand in his grip, but could not break his hold. "I would be honored . . . if a man such as Brentwood . . . made me an offer." She pushed against his chest with her free hand.

"But you wouldn't take it."

"How can you say that? You don't know me."

"But I do," he said. He released her hand and captured her chin.

"No," she whispered, recognizing his intention. He mustn't kiss her. She was weak. She had laughed with him, danced with him, kissed him, how could she resist him now?

"It's not safe is it, Susannah Bowen?" he whispered.

Warne leaned nearer. He wanted the wide mouth under his, the slim taut body closer still. He wanted the spirit she released in dance and in her free stride when she walked to be released for him. He wanted the touch of those hands, quick and light and deft.

"You are forgetting the thief," she reminded him.

"You make me forget," he answered, putting his mouth to hers, taking what he wanted.

From the moment he had clasped her hand, Warne knew he was giving up the pursuit of his enemy. Maybe the whole scheme to get Miss Lacy to Vauxhall where she might tempt the thief had been no more than a ruse to get Mrs. Bowen apart from the censorious world of London ballrooms into the dark night alone with him.

Susannah tried to pull back, but Warne's hold was unbreakable, an iron clasp. Yet not so much a clasp as a current, tugging at her, willing her to let go of her fears and reluctance. His mouth urged her to let go of her past, to plunge into the stream of feeling, letting it carry her lightly, spin her in its dizzying eddies, and wash her laughing onto some far shore.

She put her hands to the silken waistcoat, feeling his ribs with a gentle touch, and a tremor went through him.

At the touch of her hands to his ribs, Warne slanted his mouth across hers and gentled his kiss, inviting her response. And it came, reticent at first then bolder, meeting his demand as she had met his words.

The cry of a strange bird broke the stillness, and dimly he knew it for Bellaby's signal. It came again. He broke the kiss, but could not let her go. He pressed her head to the hollow under his jaw, holding her there with the fierce new longing that possessed him.

"That's Bellaby," he said. "He's found them."

She pulled back. "We must go."

It was too sudden. He struggled to master his breathing and his voice. "We must talk," he said.

"No." She stepped away from him. "This is madness."

The bird cry came again, and he offered his hand. She shook her head. He let his hand fall, and started toward the sound, listening for her footsteps behind him. At the edge of the wood, he put out his hand to stay her and looked from the shadows to the lighted path. There was Juliet Lacy, walking alone.

To his left Susannah stepped into the path, heedless of who might be watching.

"Juliet," she called.

The girl raised her head. "Susannah, hello. Sorry I wandered off. You must have been worried." She stared at Warne's coat around Susannah's shoulders.

Warne stepped into the girl's path. "Where is your friend?" he demanded.

She retreated a pace. "Gone," she said.

"Gone!" Warne cried. "Bellaby," he shouted.

Neil emerged from the shadows. "He must have come your way, Warne," he said, coming up to them.

Warne swore. He looked at Susannah Bowen, but she was regarding her cousin.

Miss Lacy stepped up to him and placed a hand on his sleeve. "Lord Warne, you needn't search for him. He will come to you soon."

"Come to me?" It was incomprehensible.

"That's his plan," Juliet said.

"Blackmail," said Bellaby.

"No!" protested Juliet. They all turned to look at her.

"Juliet," Susannah said quietly. "The man is a thief. You mustn't protect him."

"I know what he is."

"He cannot love you if he lets you risk ruin for his sake," Susannah pleaded.

"It's all right, Susannah," the girl said. "It's over. Shall we go back?"

Susannah nodded.

"You'd best give Lord Warne his coat," Juliet suggested.

17
❧❧

Two days after Lord Warne's party to Vauxhall his curricle was stolen from the street in front of White's under the very noses of the dandies in the famous window. Ann Trentfield brought the news to Evelina.

Warne's groom had apparently been distracted by a fellow servant when suddenly a young man had climbed the box and whipped the horses into motion. The cry of the startled groom alerted Lord Warne, who had been about to leave the club, and to the astonishment of all onlookers, his lordship shed his coat and pursued the vehicle on foot. By all accounts Warne would have caught the team, which was moving recklessly against traffic, except that Lord Maitland, coming upon the scene at that moment in his own phaeton, blocked the pursuit. Several other gentlemen were then obliged to keep the two men from coming to blows.

"To run the length of the street," said Mrs. Trentfield. "Lord, the man's intemperate!"

Intemperate, Susannah thought. It was just the word for him, for a man who knew the extremes of feeling. His kiss, his rage. She still did not know what had made him so, but he was the Iron Lord without doubt.

While Evelina pressed for more details of the

curricle theft, Susannah kept her head bent over her embroidery and thought of Warne, frustrated again by his elusive quarry. Not two nights before she had cost him a chance to capture his thief, and now he had been thwarted again and in a public way. He must be in a fury.

"I can't think when we've had a more scandalous season," suggested Evelina.

"I don't know, Evelina," replied her guest. "It seems to me the really good season for scandals was ten years ago." She turned to Susannah. "Wouldn't you agree, Mrs. Bowen? You were in town then, weren't you?"

Susannah nodded. "It was my come-out."

"I thought so," said Mrs. Trentfield. "Did you meet Bowen in town?"

"No," said Susannah, conscious that her stitches were suddenly too tight and puckering the cloth.

"Ah," said Mrs. Trentfield. "Evelina, did I finish telling you about Warne's curricle? It was later recovered in the Strand. The thief left behind one of Warne's cards, or perhaps he found it there." She turned to Juliet. "Didn't you meet a highwayman who gave you Warne's card?" she asked.

Susannah looked at Juliet. The color had drained from her cousin's cheeks, and her eyes had a lost look.

"Excuse me," she stammered and stood and dashed for the door.

"My dear," cried Evelina, but Juliet disappeared without turning.

"I'll go to her," Susannah said, rising. As she left the room, she heard Evelina confiding to Mrs. Trentfield that the nearer Juliet's ball drew, the more on edge the girl seemed to become.

*   *   *

Susannah found Juliet's door locked and heard the sobbing within. She tried the handle, tried pleading, and at last called, "I'll be in my room, if you need me, Juliet."

Juliet's knock came an hour later. The girl entered dry-eyed, but she did not meet Susannah's gaze. She wandered about the small room, picking up Susannah's brush, her books, her gloves. Susannah sat at the window, stitching and waiting.

"I think I will have Eastham," Juliet said. "He's dashing enough for Mama, and Papa will not be displeased." She moved from the lowboy where she had rearranged Susannah's few possessions to the mantel where she fingered a porcelain clock.

"What about you?" Susannah asked. "Does he suit you, Juliet?"

"As well him as another," Juliet said with a shrug. "I don't think there is anyone in the *ton* to suit me, truly. Eastham has courage, at least he has bottom, they all say, and he'll be proud of me because I'm pretty. We'll get on, I suppose."

"You could not love him?"

Juliet shook her head without looking Susannah's way.

Susannah thrust aside her needlework and jumped to her feet. "Then don't marry him, Juliet." She crossed to her cousin and turned Juliet around by the shoulders. "Let's talk to your papa. He must give you another season."

The blue eyes opened wide but did not brighten. "It won't matter, Susannah. I gave my heart away." She shrugged. "Eastham is probably the only one who won't notice. I'll be safe with him."

Susannah gripped her cousin's shoulders. *Safe*. The word sounded contracted, hollow, as she had become. She thought of Juliet stepping from the carriage to meet the highwayman, unafraid, ready to give herself wholeheartedly to love. How wrongheaded Susannah's guidance had been. She had been trying to protect her cousin from the dangers of love, rather than strengthening her to meet them.

She swallowed a lump in her throat. "There is Brentwood," she said dryly, coaxing a brief smile from Juliet. "I was wrong, you know," she went on. "To be safe is not enough." It was what Warne had been telling her. And if it was too late for Susannah to embrace the dangers of love, she could still restore Juliet's daring spirit. She took her cousin's hands and pressed them. "It is the highwayman you love, isn't it?"

Juliet nodded.

"Is he absolutely ineligible?"

"He won't marry me, Susannah. Not after today. He stole Lord Warne's carriage, you see. It's . . . revenge he wants." She gave a shaky sigh. "Not love, not me."

Bright tears welled in Juliet's eyes and spilled down her cheeks. She had given her heart, and the gift had been refused. Susannah took the weeping girl in her arms. Her throat ached. She would not let her cousin marry Eastham. She would convince her uncle to give Juliet another season.

Susannah's opportunity to persuade Uncle John came that very evening. Evelina went to a musicale, and Juliet was allowed to remain at home to rest up for her ball. As Susannah and Juliet were having a late supper, there was a sudden commotion in the hall. They heard doors banging, and a footman stuck his head into the breakfast room.

"What is it?" Susannah asked.

"Master's come," said the man, who then disappeared.

Susannah and Juliet rose and went to the entry.

There was Uncle John, frowning and mopping his brow. Mr. Chettle was standing to one side, holding Uncle's coat, swaying a bit, a foolish grin on his face. Mrs. Chettle was speaking quietly to the baron.

"Papa," cried Juliet. "What brings you here?"

"Your ball, Daughter," said the baron gruffly. "Wouldn't have come otherwise." He turned to Mrs. Chettle. "Remember, no fires after nine," he said. "And I do not wish to see this fellow in his cups on duty again." He shook a finger in Chettle's face.

Though Uncle John's first impression of his wife's household, which he had not visited in ten years, left him out of sorts, Mrs. Chettle, Juliet, and Susannah brought him a cold collation and established him in the small anteroom where Evelina infrequently wrote letters. He gave the room's fussy furnishings a disdainful glance, but said, "At least it's not as hot as the everlasting fire."

He summoned Susannah and listened to her report of Juliet's prospects. He had heard from Brentwood, Atwell, and Eastham, and felt satisfied that each was a suitable match for his daughter. He waited only to hear which man Susannah thought Juliet meant to have.

"None," said Susannah. She was sitting, as Uncle always liked her to do, and she wiggled her toes in her thin slippers, for the cold was numbing them.

"Speak up," her uncle demanded, though she was perfectly sure he'd heard her.

"Uncle," she said. "I think Juliet should have another season. She's a lovely girl and will have more suitors next year. She need not choose one of these three gentlemen just to make a match in a few weeks. Next spring she might choose—"

"Enough. One round of this nonsense is all she gets. Do you have any idea how much her mother has spent on gowns for the girl? Or what this ball is costing me?"

"Surely, Uncle, you—"

"No. Girls have no judgment. A bit of twaddle about love, and they run off with a half-pay officer or worse, a fellow that means no good."

Susannah stood.

"Sit down, miss," her uncle ordered.

"No, Uncle. Juliet, though she's young, has behaved well, and what mistakes she's made, she's learned from. She will be wiser next season. If there's the least chance of her happiness, Uncle, let her have it."

Uncle John glared at her. "Happiness? You think there's happiness in marriage, girl? And where does that leave you, niece? What of our bargain?"

Susannah tried not to think of the cottage with its books and walks. Her rebellious spirit had the upper hand, and she gave it free rein. "I shall make my own way in the world, Uncle, but you must not let Juliet marry now."

"Sit down," her uncle yelled.

Susannah shook her head. "Good night, Uncle John." She crossed to the door and opened it.

"We had a bargain, Susannah Lacy," Uncle John shouted. "Don't you forget it."

Susannah stepped into the hall and pulled the door shut behind her. There stood Juliet.

Susannah watched the comprehension dawn in her cousin's eyes.

"What happened to you that season, Susannah?" Juliet asked.

*   *   *

The next morning Susannah tried her aunt. Evelina rose early, and it was plain to Susannah that her aunt had not slept well. They sat in the sunny corner of the drawing room with shawls about their shoulders.

"What am I to do, dear?" Evelina asked. "The man's impossible. I am so cold, I am sure I shall take ill. And what will become of Chettle?"

Susannah soothed her aunt by suggesting that Uncle John's stay would be short.

"Thank heavens," said Evelina. "Thank goodness the cards have been sent for Juliet's ball, or the dreadful man might have cancelled it."

She explained that her husband had forced such economies on her that she would die of mortification when her friends arrived.

"And, Susannah dear, Lacy says he won't have Warne, and I can't think what I am to do. Of course I sent Warne a card, and I know he means to come. I just know Lacy will do something dreadful to embarrass us all. Would you talk to Warne, dear? Explain to him, make him see that it's impossible for him to come?"

Again Susannah found herself calming her aunt. She offered to speak to Lord Warne as soon as he arrived at the ball. When Evelina had talked herself out of the worst of her agitation, Susannah brought up the subject of Juliet's season.

"It has been wonderful, hasn't it?" Evelina said. "She's so lovely, and she has so many beaux."

"And you have enjoyed having her with you, haven't you, Aunt?" Susannah asked.

"Well yes, I have."

"Wouldn't you like her to join you again next season?"

Evelina's expression underwent a ludicrous change. Her hand flew to her chest. "Oh no," she cried. "You mustn't think of it, Niece. Lacy will cut my allowance. He'll sack Chettle. I must have my Chettle. He tells me everything."

"Nevertheless, for Juliet's sake, could you not make some adjustments?"

Susannah listened for a full half hour to the further consequences that would befall her poor aunt if Juliet were to spend another season in town. In the end she was obliged to give up and leave her aunt to compose herself. The only course left was to persuade Juliet to stand firm and refuse to marry any of the three safe suitors applying for her hand. Three days remained until Juliet's ball.

18

Kirby stared out the window of his room. In the long spring twilight, lamps were just beginning to show in the streets and windows. Tomorrow he would complete his revenge. Tonight, across town, Juliet Lacy was preparing for her come-out ball.

He gripped the top of the rough window frame and leaned his head against his arm. For him there was little left to do. He had sent a trunk with most of his possessions to the docks to be loaded on board ship, keeping only those that would help him prove his identity to his father. He had written a letter to Juliet and a message that would bring his father to the meeting place he had chosen. Tomorrow he would send them.

He should be feeling not elation, he didn't expect that, but satisfaction. He had done what he set out to do. He had kept the promise he made to himself. True, with Juliet Lacy on his mind, he had wavered the day after Vauxhall. All his delaying had been on account of her. He wished he had kissed her more often. He wished he could see her again. She had caught him off guard that night, insisting on a parting before he was ready. There were things he hadn't said.

He left the window and paced his small sitting

room. He wanted to hit something and regretted that he could not go to Hill's any longer. He would go out soon to get some supper and find a way to occupy himself until he was tired enough to sleep. His gaze fell on the pile of props he had borrowed from Mrs. Hayter—the gray wig, the mask, and the domino. He would need them one more time.

He had not seen his neighbor since the night she had offered him a bath, had not known what he would say if he did see her. He had thought about the episode more than once. He had sensed danger there, but Mrs. Hayter had shown him nothing but kindness. It made no sense that she would want him in her bed. Unless she was lonely, as Circe had been on her island, dreaming that Odysseus would someday come. The gods had ordered the hero to share the goddess's bed, and so he had.

Kirby should at least thank Mrs. Hayter for her kindness. He straightened his collar, ran a hand through his hair, and stepped across the landing to her rooms.

Her maid answered his knock and ushered him into the drawing room. In a few minutes Molly Hayter joined him, wearing the sea-green wrapper he remembered, her hair loose and tumbling down her back, her feet bare. He drew in a steadying breath.

She stood just inside the room, studying him. "You wanted to see me?" she asked.

He nodded. "I will be leaving London within two days, and I wanted to . . . thank you for . . . your help. You have been kind."

She did not move. "Yet you always run from me."

She looked hurt and vulnerable, and he thought he should offer some explanation. Maybe if he told her about Juliet Lacy, she would understand. "I . . . I'm not sure what you want from me," he said.

"A bit of company," she replied. "Is that so much?"

He shook his head.

She came into the room then and extended her hand to him. He took it, and she smiled sweetly. "I know you're hungry. You're always hungry. Will you have some meat and wine?"

"I will," he said.

She sent one of her maids to fetch a meal and drew Kirby to the scroll-ended sofa where they had sat once before. She began at once to question him, and when the wine came she poured them a glass with her own hand and watched him drink, encouraging him.

He found the wine made it easy to talk. He told her about the American cities he had thought of settling in and what he knew of them. He supposed he'd do theatre work or box until he found regular employment. She offered him more wine, and as she poured he remembered her small kindnesses. He must explain himself. He mentioned Juliet Lacy.

"Ah," said Molly. "You've fallen in love."

He put his hand to his head. He was feeling muddled. "She won't have me though," he said. "She makes her come-out tonight. She'll have some fine lord."

"Not a poor boy like you?" Molly said.

"No, never me, unless I . . . unless . . ."

Molly Hayter snatched the wine glass from the young man's suddenly slack hand and watched as he slid down the curve of the sofa and came to rest sprawled half-on, half-off the seat. For a few minutes she studied her guest's sleeping form, then rose and called for her maids. With some difficulty

Molly and the two maids eased him onto a blanket on the floor and pulled the blanket along the hall to Molly's bedroom. It was more difficult to raise the sleeping man to Molly's bed, but Molly had had enough experience with the effects of laudanum to manage. She left her maids with orders to strip the young man and went to search his rooms.

"How very thorough you are, my young lordling," she said when she found the two letters he had written. She returned to her rooms and laid the letters on her table. For an hour or more she simply read and reread each message, pacing back and forth, speaking aloud, imagining certain conversations she might have with Lord Warne and Miss Juliet Lacy. In time she stopped, arrested by an idea that had come to her.

She went to the big bed where the young man lay and pulled back the coverings from his sleeping form. He was beautiful even sprawled in drugged slumber, and she ran her fingers lightly down the warm smooth skin of his flank. He was like one of those Greeks Draycot had taken her to see, and about as lively.

"Kirby," she whispered to the sleeper, "you are like him. You refused an invitation to my bed and thought to escape. Fool."

She whirled away from him and went straight to the table and began to compose a letter of her own.

Evelina received her guests on the landing at the top of the fine painted staircase that swept up from the marble entry of her town house. The situation afforded her a view of each guest's arrival. She must spy Lord Warne's entrance before Lacy. She had stationed Susannah right behind her, though as Juliet's companion the girl hardly belonged in such a spot. Really, there was no other choice. She had been unable to bring herself to write to Lord Warne or to quarrel outright with Lacy.

There was the marquess just behind Ann Trentfield and the Chaworth-Musters. Where was Chettle? Chettle was to show his lordship into the breakfast room. She greeted the Phillipses and reached back and gave Susannah's arm an impatient squeeze.

"Susannah, dear, Warne's here. Go down at once and explain the situation to him. I don't see Chettle. Warne's coming up the stairs. Hurry, dear."

"Don't worry, Aunt, I'm going," Susannah replied. She slipped out of the niche behind her aunt and started down the crowded stairs. Lord Eastham and his friends Garrett and Newbury made way for her at the top of the stairs. She exchanged a quick greeting with one of Juliet's friends midway, and braved Ann Trentfield's cold glare as she neared the bottom. There she found Warne on the point of ascending.

"Good evening, Mrs. Bowen," he said, the warmth of his greeting unmistakable. She thought of Ann Trentfield, just above them, hearing him.

She spoke as softly as she could, inviting him to step apart with her for a moment as Evelina had something particular she wished Susannah to convey. His warm expression vanished at once, but just then a footman appeared and bowed and indicated they were to follow. He led them to the breakfast room, lit the candles in the sconces, and withdrew.

Now that they were alone Susannah found it impossible to begin. They stood just inside the door in the narrow space between the end of the table and the wall. To look at him was to recall his arms about her, his mouth on hers, and her response. She glanced up, found him watching her, and faltered.

"If I promise not to kiss you here in your aunt's house, will you find it easier to talk to me?" he asked. He rested one gloved hand on the table.

"I beg your pardon," she answered. She gripped the back of the nearest chair and straightened, raising her gaze to his. "I should not make such a piece of work of conveying a message."

"Then you haven't changed your mind about talking to me?"

She shook her head. "My aunt asked me to speak to you. With my uncle staying here, Aunt Evelina does not have the freedom she had before to . . . to invite guests to this house."

"So I am uninvited to the ball, and Lady Lacy chose you to tell me," he said. Then more slowly, "Or did you volunteer to convey my congé?"

His face had assumed its dark, rigid aspect, the iron mask in place.

"I did not volunteer, and you must understand. My aunt is entirely dependent on my uncle's good will, and he holds a grudge against you."

"Against me?"

Susannah sighed. "When you ruined your father, you also ruined mine, Uncle John's brother."

"And do you hold that against me, too?" he asked stiffly.

"No." She could not tell him that her father's ruin came after he had cast her off and that she only heard of it when it had ceased to matter.

"But you do wish me to leave Miss Lacy's ball?"

"I do," she admitted.

"Well," he said. "That's a leveller. I suppose you

know it will require an act of humility on my part. I'm not inclined to bend by nature."

She smiled at him. "I know." He flashed her a quick grin. "But you see, I've changed my mind about Juliet, and I must get Uncle to agree to another season for her."

"Changed your mind? Why?"

Your kisses. She gripped the chair back tightly. "Our . . . talks. You made me see that a safe marriage would not do for Juliet. And Juliet herself proved me wrong. She was not the fool I . . . thought she'd be."

"So you don't want her to take Eastham or Brentwood?"

"No."

"And you, Susannah? Do you want another season?" The little gap between them had diminished somehow though neither had taken a step.

He meant a real season, a season for her. She could see it in his eyes. Unthinkable, a season for her, for the constrained thing she had become. "No."

"You could marry me, Susannah Bowen. Your cousin could spend a season with us."

"What?"

"Marry me, Susannah."

She knew a mad moment of joy, followed by a sharp, wrenching pain. "I can't," she blurted. She could if he had asked knowing the truth about her, but to tell him now would be unendurable. If he no longer believed her good and decent and honest, she could not bear it.

He was watching her closely. For a moment his eyes had been bright skies of hope. Now they were shadowed.

"Well then," he said. "I'll take my leave."

She had to make him see the fault lay in her.

"You deserve a better bride, lovelier, richer, I don't know, better." Her hands fluttered up uselessly.

He caught them and held them for a long moment.

"I thought we agreed weeks ago that I would be the judge of that," he said. "Good night, Susannah."

Juliet was dancing a waltz with Lord Eastham when it occurred to her that her resolution to have him might falter in the day-to-day intimacies of marriage. His proximity, the sticky warmth of the hand at her waist, the breath mingling with hers, struck her as circumstances that might be trying to endure, particularly with the recollection of other embraces clear in her mind. Susannah's arguments began to gain unexpected force, and then there were the acrimonious scenes between her parents to which she'd been witness daily throughout the week. It was true, she had no heart to give, but she still had a mind, and she perceived that her mind was unlikely to be satisfied with Eastham. And if not with Eastham, certainly not with Brentwood, and she doubted she could please Lord Atwell in that regard.

She blushed as she came to this conclusion, realizing that the man she was waltzing with was very likely framing a proposal even as they danced and with every expectation of her delighted acceptance. She began to consider how she might disabuse him of the notion.

When the music ended, Lord Eastham said, "Miss Lacy, would you step out onto the balcony with me for a bit of air?"

"Of course," she said. She had formed no definite plan and looked round wildly for Susannah, but there was no companion to save her. Eastham was ready to pay his addresses she was sure. They strolled toward the open doors, and she thought of tripping or sneezing or pleading a headache. As they reached the doors a footman came up bearing a tray with only an envelope on it.

"Miss Lacy," he called.

She stopped. Perhaps it was from Susannah. Her cousin had seen how close she was to the trap and had sent a messenger to save her.

"Excuse me, Lord Eastham, just a moment please," she said. She lifted the envelope from the silver tray and looked at the writing. Not Susannah's, but Kirby's. Her hand trembled and she felt her heart race. She tore the missive open and scanned the words.

"He's changed his mind," she said aloud. "Oh dear, I must . . ." She looked up and found Eastham watching her, his brows drawn into a scowl.

"Oh, Lord Eastham, forgive me," she said. "I must go. Thank you for being one of my *beaux* this season. You were very . . . nice. Thank you, excuse me." She backed away from her frowning suitor, then whirled and hurried from the room.

Susannah was nowhere in sight. A quadrille was in progress. Papa was talking to Atwell; Mama, listening to Brentwood. She had perhaps a quarter of an hour to make her escape. She would just write Susannah a note. Susannah would be pleased.

Ann Trentfield had been to duller balls, but none that left her feeling quite so resentful. That that little nonentity Susannah Lacy, with her high collars and lace caps and no bosom to speak of, should command Warne, the only decent prospect on the marriage mart for a widow, was the outside of enough. And that she should pretend to respectability when she was nothing but Price's castoff was infuriating. Ann had not missed the tête-à- tête between the supposed Mrs. Bowen and Warne, and then she had not seen the marquess again.

Mrs. Chaworth-Musters came up to her friend at that moment. "Have you noticed Lacy?" she asked.

"Lacy?" Ann glanced at their host, who looked exceptionally grim and stiff. She thought Evelina very clever to have managed to live apart from the man.

"You'd think he could produce a smile for his daughter's come-out. Evelina looks terrified of him," Mrs. Chaworth-Musters pointed out.

It was then that Ann got her inspiration. "Oh, I wouldn't blame him, he's lost his convenient."

"Do tell," invited Ann's friend.

"It's obvious really. Susannah Lacy, ruined by Price, moves in with her uncle. What, ten years in Berkshire? It's a wonder that he let her come to town, knowing her character."

"She's left him for a new protector, you think?"

"Didn't you see her go off with Warne tonight?" Ann asked. "Well, he didn't come up. I suppose Lacy won't allow Warne in the house."

"Does Evelina know, do you think?" asked Mrs. Chaworth-Musters, looking at their hostess.

"That she's been harboring her husband's *cher amie*? She must not. She's so trusting."

"What can we do?"

Ann laughed. The evening was no longer dull.

19
❧❧

Juliet expected a bit of an argument from the jarvey when they reached the address she had given him. The neighborhood was far from her own fashionable street, but she stepped resolutely from the hackney and offered the man a brisk thank you and what she hoped was a generous gratuity.

"Miss," he called after her, but she pulled her cloak tightly around her ball gown and hurried up the steps to the lodging house. The door was open, and light and laughter poured out from the lower rooms. She paused briefly, waved at the still-waiting driver, and stepped inside.

"Oh ho, what have we here?" said a tall, stout man from an open door. He swayed toward her and rocked back unsteadily on his heels. "Draycot, are you expecting a princess?" the tall man shouted to someone within.

"I'm expected upstairs," Juliet said quickly and dashed past the man as he tilted toward her again.

"Hey!" he called, but she tripped lightly up the stairs, slowing her steps only when it appeared the tall man would not follow. She wound her way up to the third story where Kirby's letter indicated he had his rooms. On the landing there were two doors, and the one on the right was open.

She stuck her head in and found a comfortable

drawing room, far more opulent than what she had imagined his lodgings to be. "Kirby?" she called. She heard a muffled "hello" and turned to the sound. A hall led away from the drawing room to the rear of the suite.

She headed toward the sound. Another door was open at the end of the hall, and she could see the glow of lamplight on a fine carpet. It struck her as she reached this far door that the way had been made too easy as it is in the fairy tale when the princess finds the spindle and pricks her finger. But she crossed the threshold and then it did not matter, for there on a richly hung bed lay Kirby, stripped and sprawled, ominously still.

With a cry she ran to him, and she scarcely registered the door shutting behind her or the key turning in the lock. *He breathed.*

Susannah did not return to the ballroom at once. Warne had stunned her, and it took some moments for the turmoil of regret and wonder to subside. She paced the breakfast room restlessly, until she recalled Juliet's situation. Then, admitting to herself that she was hiding, she left the little room. In the hall, she encountered Mrs. Chettle, who begged Susannah's help directing the setting out of the food in the supper room.

When she finally did return to the ball, she saw Eastham take a terse leave of Uncle John. She looked for Juliet but did not see her. Juliet must have refused him, and Susannah's spirits lifted. There was hope after all.

"Where is your charge, miss?" Uncle John demanded, coming up to Susannah. "You put her up to this, I warrant, and you'll pay. Find her."

Susannah bowed and went in search of her cousin, not to bring her back as Uncle John wished but to keep Juliet from further encounters with her suitors. But Juliet was not in any of the rooms set aside for the guests, not even the ladies' retiring room. The girl wasn't in her bedroom either. There Susannah felt the first hint of alarm. Juliet's wardrobe hung open, a piece of carelessness Aunt Evelina's abigail never committed. She was gone, the voice of alarm whispered, but Susannah could not believe it.

It was too like her own elopement. She had gone in her gown and slippers from the Ravenswood ball to Price's hired chaise and her inevitable ruin. Perhaps Juliet had missed her below and come looking for her. She turned to her own room. A lamp was lit on her sewing table and tucked under it was a piece of pressed paper. Even before she picked it up, she knew what the brief message would tell her. Juliet had gone to her highwayman. Love had conquered reason, propriety, and prudence. And if the man did not love Juliet in return, she would be ruined.

Susannah could not help emitting a cry of anguish. It must not be. Her cousin must not suffer as she had. She took up the little note and read it again. He had not come to the house. Juliet was going to him somewhere in town. Susannah grabbed her own cloak and warmer gloves. She took the servants' stair and went in search of Chettle. Someone must have helped Juliet get away. If the girl went by hack, someone might know what address Juliet had given the jarvey.

Halfway down the stairs a vision came to her that sapped her limbs of strength. She sat down hard and willed her legs to stop trembling. But the memory could not be dispelled. In a room in an inn on the Great North Road, Price had shown her how very ungallant a man could be. She had still believed he meant to marry her and had not screamed or fought him, and over the years that had hurt most of all.

Susannah told herself that Juliet's highwayman was not Price; still she did not want to go after them alone. She wanted Warne, and Warne must help her. He had encouraged Juliet's meetings with the man.

A disapproving butler showed Susannah into Warne's library. Warne stood at the mantel, leaning an elbow on the marble shelf, staring down into the fire. He straightened when she entered, but made no move toward her.

"Did I conjure you?" he asked, setting aside a glass of amber liquid he held in one hand. "I must have. Can I offer you some refreshment?"

She shook her head. "I need your help," she said.

"It's yours."

"Juliet's gone to meet your thief."

He swore and crossed the room to her. "When?" he demanded.

"Perhaps an hour ago," Susannah answered. "She left me this note." Susannah held it out to him, and as he scanned it, she said, "I know the address she's gone to. I talked to the footman who handed her into the hack."

Warne strode to the bellpull and gave it a vicious tug. "We need Bellaby." When the butler reappeared, Warne ordered him to send two footmen in search of his friend. Then he turned back to Susannah, and she tried to compose her face. "Blame me in this and not yourself. Believe me I will do what I can to see that Miss Lacy is not ruined by this night."

"If I had helped you catch the man . . ." She feared it was true. Her distrust of Warne had kept her from aiding him until it was too late.

He took her hands. "Do not blame yourself for my failure."

"As you are blaming yourself for mine?" She ventured a smile.

"Damn," he said, running his thumbs across the backs of her hands, his eyes searching hers. "You wouldn't reconsider my offer?"

She averted her gaze. The fire burned steadily in the hearth, its hiss and snap the only sound in the room. *Trust,* she told herself. "There are things you don't know. Lies. I am not . . ."

Warne waited, suspended, clasping her hands, willing her to trust him, to continue.

A knock interrupted them. They stepped apart, and Pedrick entered. "Another visitor, my lord," he announced. A Mrs. Hayter. She offers this card and insists that you will see her."

Warne took the card and held it out to Susannah. She wanted to question him, but his face had become a mask of hatred. He strode to a door in the opposite wall, opened it, and motioned for Susannah to step into the next room. "Wait here," he told her. "You wanted to know what made the Iron Lord? Listen."

Susannah slipped into the darkened room and stood where the door was left ajar.

Warne retied his cravat and donned his coat. His visitor was ushered in. Time had hardly altered her, he thought. She was a serpent in a woman's body, fine white skin, green eyes, deep red hair, and indolent motion—beauty and malice. And she would make a game of it, a nasty game, whatever she came for.

"Good evening, my lord." She strolled past him, her scent coiling round him in her wake, and ran her fingers along one of the shelves. "Nice library." She stopped and pulled out a book and let it fall open. "Cut pages, too. Not like your father's library, after all. He had things other than books to amuse him."

"What have you come for, Molly?"

"I have something of yours, Warne," she said, looking at him slyly, her hands stroking the book.

"I doubt it."

"But you saw the card?"

"Where did you get it, Molly? Maitland?" He watched her moves.

"Straight from the thief, my proud lord. Stole your rig the other day, didn't he?" She came up to him then. "I can lead you right to him. For a price."

"That was always your way," he said, holding back the rage building inside him. He wanted to shake her, so he put his hands in his pockets and balled them into fists.

"Yes. It is my way. It has to be. Men are all cheats and liars, as you are, as your father was. You owe me."

"I owe you," he shouted, unable to contain his fury.

She turned from him and slammed the book down on a table. "You were glad enough to learn from me, my too-proud lord. Every day. And your father put a gold boy aside for me for everything I taught you, but I didn't get the blunt. You ran away with your milk and water bitch, and when your father went to bring you back, your mother kicked me out. All my work for nothing. I got nothing and no one."

"You trusted my father. That was your mistake, Molly."

She shrugged. "I intend to make up for that

tonight. I want ten thousand pounds, my lord."

He laughed. "You will be in hell a long time before I pay you such a sum."

"I don't think so, Lord Warne." She was suddenly serious. "You see, I have your Miss Lacy in a most compromising position for a young lady. She and your thief are intimately acquainted, you might say."

He was careful to show no reaction. She had assumed as most of the *ton* did, that he was one of Juliet's suitors. This was her revenge, this holding something over him, but he already knew of the link between the thief and Juliet. The puzzle was how Molly Hayter had come to know it, or to claim that she had Miss Lacy. Was she behind the thief's actions? It made little sense. He knew her indolence and doubted she would have troubled herself to arrange the thief's attacks on him. Besides, she could have acted against him any time in the last few years.

"Ah," said Warne. "The ten thousand pounds is for your silence?"

She nodded.

"And how am I to be sure that you have Miss Lacy?"

"You must accompany me to—"

"—Tavistock Street?" He named the street Susannah had gleaned from the Lacy footman.

She started and made a recovery. "You should have called on me, Warne, if you knew the place. Other gentlemen have."

"How do I know Miss Lacy is there?"

"She came straight from the ball in her white gown with roses in her hair."

"And why not apply to her parents in the matter of her return?"

Again he drew a reaction, a quick change in her expression that told him she was holding something back. She laughed, and he thought how very cruel a sound some laughter could be. "I told you. I have something of yours, and I want to show it to you. Really, it's quite generous of me."

It was a riddle he could not solve, and he wondered if she were a little mad, or if she had a pistol. She had not removed her cloak, and she must have anticipated some resistance from him. Bellaby would be here soon. If Warne could keep her talking and get her to face him with her back to the door. "And if I don't want to pay your price?" he asked.

"The girl will be exposed and ruined, and I promise you, Warne, your name will come into it."

He turned away from her, strolling slowly toward his desk, drawing her gaze, speaking over his shoulder. "You must know, Molly, that your visit is unexpected. I haven't such a sum about me." He took his empty hands from his pockets and held them out. "Perhaps you should come back another day." He thought he heard a door open.

"I think not, Warne, I will get what I want."

"How?" he asked bluntly, striding straight toward her.

"This way," she said and drew a little pistol. He checked.

Behind her the study door opened, and Bellaby entered.

"Warne, what the devil!"

Warne kept his eyes on Molly Hayter's. The instant her gaze flickered away from him, he lunged, grabbing her wrist, twisting and squeezing, until she screamed and dropped the gun. Her other hand came up to claw his eyes, and he seized it and wrenched it down. Bellaby picked up the fallen gun and levelled it at Molly.

"Here now, ma'am, be still," he ordered.

Molly looked at him with a sneer, but ceased her struggles.

"Who is she?" Bellaby asked.

"Molly Hayter," said Warne.

"The maid," he said. "And you haven't killed her yet?"

"No," Warne answered. "We're going to pay a visit to Molly's lodging, but first Molly, I want you to meet Mrs. Bowen, who is a witness to your extortion attempt." He crossed to the door he'd left ajar for Susannah.

She entered as he said her name, and he reached out and took her hands. Her face was drawn with worry, and he whispered, "Let's go find Juliet."

20

The chaise halted in the pre-dawn blackness outside a dark, brick-fronted building of severe
Palladian design. Warne did not have to prod Molly Hayter to lead the way. She descended from the
carriage, swept up the few steps, and entered the
building. From the moment he'd disarmed her, she
had been all acquiescence, and he could not escape
the feeling that he was playing into her hands. Her
smug unconcern was a sign she had some further
trick planned.

They passed a first-floor apartment where several
stuporous gentlemen sat among empty wine bot-
tles, and climbed until they reached the third story. "My humble rooms, my lord marquess," Molly
said, indicating an open door with a sweep of her
arm. "You'll find what you're looking for in my
bed."

Susannah flashed him a quick apprehensive
glance, and he tightened his grip on her arm,
ushering her into the entry. Molly followed with
Bellaby behind her. The small vestibule opened
on an opulent drawing room, definitely in Molly's
style. "Where?" Warne demanded.

"Down that hall," Molly answered.

Before he could caution her, Susannah dashed
ahead, calling for Juliet.

The girl's voice answered from behind the far door. "We're in here."

Susannah tried the door. "It's locked."

"The key," he said to Molly.

She grinned then. "Of course, my lord marquess." She pulled the strings of her reticule, fished in the small bag, and produced a key. He snatched it from her and applied it to the lock. The door swung inward.

He entered and halted abruptly. The room was cold and smelled faintly of sour wine. Juliet Lacy stood at the foot of a large bed, looking as if she had just left the ballroom. But beside her, leaning weakly, half-supported by the disordered bed, coatless, his shirt hanging out, only one foot booted, was a youth who might have been Warne himself.

Sounds rang hollowly in his ears. Susannah Bowen gasped. Bellaby cried, "My God!" And Molly Hayter laughed.

The young man straightened. His face was ashen as if he'd been ill, but his eyes regarded Warne with burning anger.

"Who are you?" Warne demanded. He took two steps and stopped, his feet suddenly too heavy to move.

"Francis Kirby Arden," the pale youth said. He shivered in the draft from an open window.

"It's a trick," Warne cried.

"Nae, no trick," the youth answered, his voice an echo of Warne's.

"It must be," Warne protested. He thought he must be mad. "Ellen died in January of '97. I saw the grave. The sexton gave me her ring."

Something flickered in the boy's gaze. "She died in February of '13 of a fever."

Susannah was no more than an arm's length from

Warne, but she knew she must not touch him. He and the boy stood frozen, like two of Elgin's marbles, carved by the same hand.

Warne struggled to make sense of the truth before his eyes. How fate had mocked him. His young bride had not died. He had a son. He couldn't take it in. He had thought the wounds of that time no longer pained him, but his chest suddenly ached. Ellen had lived for sixteen years and never sought him. "She didn't come to me?"

Anger flared in the blue eyes that matched his own. "You abandoned her. You abandoned . . ." The boy took an unsteady step toward Warne, his fists clenched.

"No," Warne answered. "I was . . ." he broke off, unwilling to describe the humiliation of his own youth to this hard-eyed young man.

Bellaby stepped forward. "Your grandfather put him in chains, boy," he declared hotly.

The young man's bleak gaze shifted to Bellaby then back to Warne. After a moment the youth said, "Mother feared the old marquess. She was waiting for him to die."

It was a concession, Warne thought. But the old man didn't die soon enough. Ellen must have escaped his father, hidden herself somewhere. "Where were you born?"

"Stratford," the boy said. "In September of '97." He struggled to stand proud. "My christening is in the church records," he added defiantly.

It was the only time a son of his and Ellen Kirby's could have been born. And the place was one that only his scholarly Ellen would choose. She had given birth to her Arden where the son of Mary Arden had lived.

"And then?" he asked, his voice less harsh, as

he watched the young man who claimed to be his son.

"We moved from place to place. When I was six, we came to Glenryn near Dumfries. Mother got a situation there as a housekeeper."

He forced himself to ask. "And when she died?"

"I joined a traveling theatre company and worked my way here." It was a proud answer.

Molly Hayter laughed again. She strolled to the fireplace, tugging at her gloves. "Ask him what he was doing in London, my fine lord. In my bed."

"Oooh, of all the shabby tricks," Juliet Lacy interjected. She strode forward, taking a stand beside the youth. "He was drugged," she said pointedly.

Warne cast a savage glance at Molly. She shrugged. "This time. There was no laudanum the last time you came to my bed, was there, Kirby?"

The young man looked at her for the first time. "I trusted you. I thought you were a friend."

Bellaby snorted. "Blackmailing b—"

"Bellaby," Warne said sharply. He needed time to think. The events of the last month were tumbling in his mind, rearranging themselves in a new pattern. The handwriting on his cards had been familiar because it was so like Ellen's. The bitter, resentful boy before him had not attacked his business interests because the boy had known only the scandals attached to Warne's name and had wanted only to prove what Warne had been ignorant of—their kinship. There was, as he had guessed, no mercenary motive in the thief's acts—only revenge.

But Molly Hayter had not been part of the plan. No doubt she had seen and recognized the boy. The boy did not know her role in Warne's past and had not arranged this meeting. At Vauxhall Juliet Lacy had said the thief would come to him. You abandoned, the boy had said. He had not said *me*, but Warne knew he meant it. He knew what he would want from such a father—to make that father suffer humiliation and powerlessness and rejection.

He kept his gaze fixed on the youth. "I know what . . . Kirby was doing in London. He was avenging himself on the father his boyhood lacked." At the words of the old story Kirby stiffened, a sudden alertness in his eyes.

Warne felt his heart constrict. This was Ellen's son. He searched his mind for the rest of the passage where the boy Telemakhos meets his father for the first time. "No other Odysseus will ever come," he said.

The words seemed to stir some inner struggle in Kirby. His frame shook. "You never looked again. You lived in your fine house while she . . . labored for fools who thought themselves above her. You spent thousands of pounds while she made shillings. She was so good . . ." his voice faltered. ". . . and you took mistresses."

Warne said nothing. He was suddenly conscious of Susannah Bowen at his side. She had reawakened his heart. He would not be feeling the boy's pain if he had not come to love Susannah. Even now when she was silent he felt her warm sympathy for him and for the boy. Susannah, to whom he hoped to offer his name, free of the past, but perhaps a man was never free of the past.

Kirby went on. "I know it all. Her father wrote to her, and she saved every scrap of news about you."

"Did she send you to me?" Warne asked.

Again Kirby's eyes gave away the battle raging

inside him. "She made me promise I would present myself to you." It was plain the boy had intended to do just that and walk away.

Warne let a long moment pass. "You're free then, aren't you," he suggested gently. He wanted to save his son from the hatred that had consumed his own life. Already the boy was fortunate. He had Juliet Lacy by his side. "Unless you would like something more from me."

Kirby's blue eyes narrowed warily, but he turned to Juliet, and put his arm around her waist in an unmistakably possessive gesture. "I want to marry Miss Lacy."

Warne nodded with swift comprehension. "So, you need to be my son, and heir, to have Miss Lacy for a bride?"

Kirby remained silent. Juliet Lacy gave his arm a tug, and the two exchanged a look. It was apparent there was some agreement between them that had to be honored. Warne waited.

It was a long wait, some final resistance holding Kirby silent. "I will be your son, if you will have me," he said at last.

"Even if you must be Earl of Dovedale?" Warne asked. "I suspect you'll have to take the title to get Lord Lacy's approval for this match."

Then Molly Hayter laughed. "How affecting! Father and son reconciled. You'll never get Lacy's approval. You think Byron was disgraced. What a story I'll have to tell about this little father-son war and the girl ruined between you. Who had her first?"

"Witch," Kirby yelled and sprang at her. He drove Molly against the wall and held her pinned there, a shaking forearm across her throat.

Warne reached them in two quick strides. "She

won't do any talking, Kirby," he told his son, gently pulling the boy off their enemy. "I promise you."

Kirby stumbled back, his energy drained by the sudden outburst. His knees buckled and Bellaby rushed forward to catch the boy under one arm and shoulder his weight. Warne exchanged a glance with his friend and saw that Bellaby understood him. It was time to get the others home so that he could deal with Molly.

"Ladies," Bellaby said. "In case you've forgotten, this is a rescue. Follow me."

When they had gone, Warne faced Molly Hayter. "You betrayed us to my father, didn't you, Molly," he said, surprised that he felt no desire to hit her. "You're the one."

"Your father promised to pay well." She rubbed her injured throat and regarded him sullenly.

Warne glanced at the luxuries of the room. "If he didn't, others did. What do you know about money, Molly?"

"How to get it and spend it," she told him.

"Do you know how to use it to destroy another's fortune? I do. You have a week to get out. Follow Byron and Brummell to the Continent."

"And if I don't?"

"*No score left unpaid*. I'll ruin you, Molly, and any protector you take."

"I hate you."

Warne smiled. A bit of revenge was satisfying after all. "Don't you know, Molly, the gods punished the nymph for clinging to the hero." He turned and strode from the room.

Her voice came after him down the hall. "I had him, Warne. I had your son. What if he's got a son on me? Then I'll have something of yours, Warne."

At the door he stopped and glanced back at the woman trailing after him. "Good day, Molly. One week."

They descended from Warne's carriage under overcast skies. A bitter wind pressed Susannah's cape around her, making her appear vulnerable. He held her hand a moment longer than was strictly necessary. He had wanted to take her hand in the carriage but so much remained unresolved between them.

He had set Bellaby down at the house on Upper Brook Street to begin the steps necessary to secure Kirby's position as Lord Dovedale. Now it was his plan to have a private word with Lord Lacy, assuring him of his daughter's safety and Kirby's honorable intentions. Arranging this marriage would be the first thing he could do for his son, and he wanted to achieve it without delay. He would persuade Lacy to accept the boy's suit. Then he would ask for just a few words with Susannah Bowen. She looked exhausted, but he wanted to let her know that he would marry her, whatever secrets she had.

The ladies were shivering before a footman could be roused to answer the door. He took one startled look at them and disappeared into the house. Juliet Lacy started forward when her father appeared, striding toward them, a wrapper around his evening clothes, a nightcap on his head. He filled the doorway, his robe flapping about him in the wind.

"My girl, what have you done?" he demanded of his daughter. His narrow gaze swung to Susannah. "Away, hussy," he yelled. "Be gone. You've disgraced this house."

"Papa," said Juliet. "Susannah came to find me."

"She's a wanton, a whore." He came out onto

the steps, his hands shooing Susannah away. She retreated, shock and pain in her eyes. Warne caught her and clasped her to his side, trying to understand Lacy's accusations.

"I took you in, Susannah Lacy, when you sinned with Price. Ten years I gave you shelter when you were no more than a stale. Ingratitude. Drag my name into it. Bridewell is too good for you, hussy. Go. Go. Walk the streets."

Warne put Susannah behind him, holding her firmly. "Enough," he commanded. "Calm yourself, Lacy. Mrs. Bowen has been maligned."

"She's not Mrs. Bowen. She never married. Soiled goods. No man would have her then, or now."

"Enough, I say," Warne repeated. "Whatever her name, she is above reproach. We will clear up any misunderstanding about her reputation."

"I will not have her in this house."

"Let me go. Please, Lord Warne," Susannah pleaded, pulling away from him.

"No." He gripped her arm tightly. He would not let her give in to her mad uncle's ravings. "What is being said against her? By whom?"

"I refuse to answer that question," said Lacy. "And that's my daughter, sir. Come in at once, Juliet."

"Papa, no. Why are you doing this to Susannah?" Juliet cried.

"Do not be deceived by her, girl. Get that woman out of my sight," he shouted.

"Mrs. Bowen rescued your daughter tonight, sir," said Kirby quietly.

"Who are you?" demanded Lacy.

"Francis Arden." Kirby cast a quick glance at Warne. "Earl of Dovedale. I intend to marry your daughter, sir."

"Marry my daughter?" Lacy looked from Kirby to Warne, incredulity and resentment giving way to a calculating gleam in his eyes. "Then take that woman away."

An icy blast of wind hit them, and Susannah shivered. Warne felt a hot, dry rage threaten to consume him in spite of the cold. He held it in check. He was momentarily powerless to spare Susannah the humiliation of Lacy's words. He could see now how her proud spirit had been subdued in her uncle's house. He helped her to his carriage and settled her inside.

"Coachman will take you to Brook Street. Bellaby's there, and my housekeeper will find a place for you to rest. We will clear up this false story. Wait for me," he urged her. There was a blind look in her eyes that he did not trust, and he wanted to kiss her but not with her uncle frowning down on them. He stepped back and waved the coachman on.

Susannah was very cold. She kept her teeth clenched and her arms crossed tightly. Still she was shaking deep inside. If she tried to speak or move the shaking would break her apart. She could not go to his house to wait for him.

It was light now, and other carriages were about. Once or twice, the driver slowed to let another vehicle pass. Susannah uncrossed her arms and pulled herself over to the door. She tapped on the roof as loudly as she could. The carriage slowed, then stopped. She pushed open the door. She felt lightheaded, and the shivering was beginning to take over her limbs. She would never get away if she hesitated now. She gathered her cloak about her and jumped down, hitting the pavement hard and taking a couple of stumbling steps. The driver yelled, but she hurried away.

When Susannah reached Holburn, she thought of Henry and turned her steps toward his lodging. Then it started to snow, a freak storm. She walked on.

Now it was complete. The past had reclaimed them both. Winter had returned.

21

The snow hushed the city. Susannah sat at the window of Henry's rooms watching the streets fill up with white. Only a few incongruously green leaves remained visible on the trees across the way. She had stopped shivering except for a tiny quiver somewhere deep inside. Her brother had wrapped her in an extra counterpane and supplied her with hot coffee or tea whenever her cup cooled. He had taken her in without question, he and Ned Noakes sensing her need for quiet. Ned had somehow procured most of her things from the Lacys', and she had had time to think.

Twice in her life she had come to London, fallen in love, and been ruined. She did not wonder much at this second downfall. Someone had seen her go apart with Warne last night, had seen them dance at Almack's, had remembered her shameful past. Warne would soon know the whole history and be grateful that she had not accepted his offer. He was not bound to her in any way.

The unseasonal storm would close the roads and prevent the stage from running, but soon, maybe tomorrow, she would leave London for Bath. There was an employment agency there always in need of people to fill temporary positions with visitors to the city. Once, when she had thought herself unable to bear another week in her uncle's house, Susannah had talked to the couple who ran the agency. She would present herself to them now and hope they could help her.

Warne returned to the house on Upper Brook Street in the early dark of that snowy day. He found his friend and his son in his library. He greeted them, and saw a look pass between the two.

"Mrs. Bowen is resting?" he asked.

"She never arrived here," Bellaby explained. "I didn't expect her. Kirby interviewed your coachman. The man says she jumped from the chaise and took off on foot."

For a moment Warne succumbed to a weary blackness. He sank into a chair and pressed his hands to his tired head. He had lost her. He had a sharp image of the figure with the unseeing gaze huddled in his carriage.

"She must have gone to her brother," Bellaby suggested.

Warne lifted his head and glanced appreciatively at Neil. Susannah was sensible, like Neil. She would do that. He thought of her quick stride, her pleasure in that small freedom. The morbid fear that seized him passed. "Yes," he said.

"Then you can find the brother and call on her tomorrow," Bellaby said. "Gray's Inn, right?"

Warne nodded.

"Kirby's told me a bit of what happened. Forced Lacy to see reason about the boy, did you?"

Warne glanced at his son, and received a look in return so like one of his own that it left him momentarily speechless. Bellaby laughed. Warne said, "Lord Lacy found that his daughter was about to make a far more ambitious marriage than he had ever dreamed of for her, and he thought it to his own advantage to consent."

"It's going to be a grand wedding, I hear," Bellaby said.

"The grandest," Warne agreed.

"But we have to wait near six months for it," Kirby said, frowning.

Bellaby reached across a playful fist and nudged the boy. Warne noted the two seemed to have come to some understanding.

"Announcement in the *Chronicle*?" Bellaby wondered.

"Tomorrow," Warne said.

"That soon?"

Warne thought it sounded far away when he recalled that he could not search for Susannah until then. He stared at the fire.

Bellaby recounted the steps he had taken on Kirby's behalf. Warne's solicitor would be calling in the morning, and the boy would be properly established in no time.

"And what of Mrs. Bowen?" Bellaby asked.

"I wanted to kill Lacy," Warne confessed. He looked at his son. "But it would be a bit awkward to kill my daughter-in-law's papa." He stood and crossed to the brandy decanter, poured himself a glass, and returned to his chair. "When Lacy separated from his wife ten years ago, the children went with him and he took Susannah in as an unpaid governess. She had run away with a fellow named Price, a half-pay officer, a notorious seducer. Price took her as far as an inn in Baldock. I suspect he raped her. At any rate he abandoned her. Her family cast her off and never made any attempt to go after the man."

He felt his body tighten in anger as he related the

story Lacy had just imparted to him, and he paused for a moment to drink a swallow of brandy, letting the fiery liquid warm him.

"Within four years her father was ruined, and shortly after, he killed himself and his wife in a driving accident. He was drunk. The eldest son has repaired the family fortune somewhat by an advantageous marriage. Lacy himself feels he was extraordinarily generous to his disgraced and penniless niece.

"This spring Lacy offered her a bargain. If she would guide Juliet to a marriage he could approve of, he would pension Susannah off with a thousand pounds and a cottage. But last night at Miss Lacy's ball, someone suggested that Susannah had been his mistress for all these years and that she was leaving his protection for mine."

"Damn," said Bellaby. "Who spread such a lie?"

"Ann Trentfield," Warne answered. "I had an interview with Mrs. Trentfield this afternoon. She is going to put her considerable powers of invention to work to repair Mrs. Bowen's reputation with the *ton*."

"Then you'll cut out her tongue," said Neil.

Warne allowed himself a grim smile. Price and Susannah's father were beyond his anger. Lacy was to become a family connection. So Ann Trentfield had borne the heat of his wrath, even if, as a gentleman, he could not strike her. But he was wiser now than he had been when his father separated him from Ellen Kirby. He would not waste his energies in fury. He would spend all to get Susannah Bowen back.

The business of establishing Francis Kirby Arden as Earl of Dovedale and legitimate offspring of the

Marquess of Warne consumed most of the day. Still Warne had found time to procure two documents he believed essential to the winning of Susannah Bowen. Then when he found her brother, he learned that she had taken the stage for Bath that morning. He returned to Brook Street, ordered a horse saddled, and went to find his son.

Kirby and Neil were in the breakfast room, looking at the ordnance survey, Neil obviously explaining something to the younger man. He broke off as Warne entered.

"Susannah took the stage for Bath this morning. I'm going after her," Warne told them.

Bellaby nodded.

"Kirby," Warne began and stopped. He wanted to marry Susannah immediately, but how could he tell his son? "I asked your mother to marry me when we were eight. I asked her again at twelve. I persuaded her to marry me at sixteen, and I never married while she lived."

Kirby studied his father. The man was not the dissolute aristocrat on whom he had imagined avenging himself. Bellaby's stories were acquainting him with this real father of his, the man his mother had loved. She was gone. No Penelope for this Odysseus. He now realized that she had waited when perhaps she should have acted.

"Father," he said. He liked the suprised look he caught in Warne's eyes. "I have something I think you could use."

The young man disappeared, and Warne turned to his friend. "What have you been telling him?" he asked.

Bellaby shrugged. "Just . . . stories." He added, "I like the boy."

Kirby returned and handed Warne a bit of folded

black cloth. "I'd take two pistols," he suggested.

Bellaby went to the map, pointing. "Look, the stage will stop here, here, and here. Should be able to catch them past Hungerford," he said. He turned, but Warne was gone.

It was a clear day, and the snow was melting. Still it was odd to see the countryside blanketed with white while the hedges and trees showed green where the wind had shaken them free of snow. The freak storm had been a source of conversation among the passengers on the stage for many tedious miles. The Meek sisters, Miss Meek and Miss Sarah Meek, two ladies who shared a vicarage with their brother near Bath, could not recall anything like it. Susannah suspected they were starved for excitement. They feared for their roses and their brother, who, according to their account, was hopelessly unable to do for himself, and must have frozen somewhere between the church and the vicarage without his sisters there to keep him dressed sensibly. The farmer and his wife, with whom Susannah shared her seat, had also been deeply concerned by the snow. There were crops newly sprouted which surely had been blasted by the cold. Only the pockmarked man in the corner opposite hers seemed indifferent to the weather. "It's not the end of the world," he said early in the conversation, and closed his eyes.

Susannah tried to adopt his phlegmatic approach. *It's not the end of the world*, she told herself. But the farmer's restless little boy stood clinging to his father's legs and from time to time would clutch

Susannah's knee and smile shyly at her, or one of the Miss Meeks would say something about their brother, and Susannah would feel the shivering start inside her again. She reminded herself that she was very strong, that for ten years her self-sufficiency had sustained her in Uncle John's cold house. And she would have better memories to sustain her in this exile. Warne's kiss and his touch.

She was thinking of his warm grasp that night as they made their way through the woods of Vauxhall, when the horses suddenly slowed and the farmer clutched his son to keep the boy from falling.

"We've been stopped," said Miss Meek.

"Likely a fallen tree or sommat," said the pock-marked man, rousing himself and taking a look out the window.

But this prosaic view was contradicted when a shot rang out, followed by the shouts of the driver and some other party.

"Highwaymen!" breathed Miss Sarah Meek, her eyes round with excitement.

Susannah wanted to suggest that being held up was an overrated experience, but the door of the stage was wrenched open, and a voice came from outside, calling her name. "No one will be harmed if Mrs. Bowen steps out of the coach," said the voice.

Her fellow travellers regarded her as if she had sprouted a second head. None of them would come to her aid, nor did she wish them to offer any resistance to an armed ruffian.

"Susannah Bowen," the deep, muffled voice called again.

"Excuse me," she said to the others. "It appears I must get out here. I'm sure you will all be safe." She mustered what dignity she could and stepped from the carriage.

Then she had to smile. It was silly really. It could not be happening, and he looked very dangerous. He wore the tricorn, the black mask over his face, a greatcoat with an impressive number of capes, and held a pistol braced across his saddle horn. The blue eyes, however, were laughing.

"What do you want with me, sir?" she asked.

He leaned down and said softly, "Do you want me to tell you *here*?"

She glanced back at the stage and saw her fellow passengers gaping at them. She shook her head.

"Then you'll have to come with me, Susannah," he said. "There's a stump over there you can mount from, but first . . ." With his free hand he reached behind him and untied a bundle from the back of his horse. He handed it to her. "For your fellow travellers."

Susannah passed the bundle, which smelled suspiciously like fresh bread, into the stage.

"Will you be safe, ma'am?" the farmer asked, taking it from her hands.

"I doubt it," said Susannah. "But I will be happy," she assured them. She turned away from the stage, and was about to shut the door when Warne leaned down and tossed a white card into the passengers' midst.

The Meek sisters were puzzling over its meaning many miles later, for the little card read *The Marquess of Warne*.

"That was hardly original," Susannah complained later when they had been shown to a private room at the Bear, an inn on the outskirts of Hungerford. A fire was blazing and a table had been set for them, yet she stood a little apart from him looking at the flames.

"Remember," he said softly. "I did it first. Kirby merely copied me."

She sensed that he had closed the distance between them, but she did not look up. She wasn't sure how he would look at her now that he knew, as he undoubtedly did, that she was not Susannah Bowen.

"You called me Mrs. Bowen this afternoon," she said.

"I thought you would be travelling under that name," he replied mildly. "But you needn't use it any longer if you don't wish to."

She glanced up then, caught the full light in his eyes, and blinked. "You cannot wish to marry me, knowing what you must know," she said flatly. "I've been ruined twice."

He smiled at that. She was a babe really, who hardly knew all the ways he meant to ruin her. "But I do wish to marry you," he said. He saw the wild incredulity in her eyes, and his throat ached for the hurt she had suffered. "Your uncle is a passionless man. The words he used against you could be said of Molly Hayter, not you. The words for you are different. Do you want to hear them?"

Susannah shook her head. Her eyes stung with tears, and she turned her back to him. After a moment she felt his hands on her shoulders turning her around, and she had no power to resist his gentleness. She let herself be folded in a quiet embrace, her face pressed to his shoulder, his hand cradling her head.

"I'll say them anyway, my love," he whispered. "I am rather used to having my way. Generous," he began. "Kind, witty, honest, honorable . . ."

"Stop," she protested, lifting her head, but that proved to be a mistake, and she saw it at once. He went still, and the quality of his embrace changed.

After a moment he seemed to master himself and took her by the hand, pulling her to the table set for them. From his coat he withdrew two papers and spread them on the linen. "Look," he said. "Ruin's reward."

Susannah bent over the two official-looking documents. The language of the first had to do with title and boundaries, and she recognized it as a deed to the cottage her uncle had promised her. She glanced at Warne.

"The second one," he said.

The second was easier to read, the language more plain, though still official. It granted the bearer the right to marry at any convenient time or place, a special license. He was offering her safety or the danger of his love, letting her choose.

She raised her eyes to his. She seemed to be standing on a high bluff, one she must step off. "I love you," she said.

He pulled her to him and reached for her cap, his fingers tearing at the pins.

"What are you doing?" she managed to ask.

He plucked the lace cap from her and tossed it on the fire. It curled and blackened instantly and disappeared in a little flare of light. "I would rather you not wear caps anymore," he said and his mouth descended on hers.

She yielded to him, and he felt the fear in her dissolve.

If he had given the first half of his life to hatred, he would give the second half to love. He would not make iron only, but flesh and blood, not machines but sons . . . and daughters . . . with wide mouths and straight backs and fiery hair like their mother's. The Iron Lord lifted his head and looked in the generous eyes of his love and he laughed.